HUNTER AND MASTER

A man waits for me in the light of the mountaintop.

No, not a man. Antlers rise from his head. A tail, like a lion's tail, sweeps the ground behind him. He stands on hooves and his legs are as shaggy as the legs of the bison. His hands are tipped with claws like the claws of a cat.

He stares at me and I recognise the look in his eyes. He was the spirit in the young buck. He was the leader of the wolf pack. He was the snake and the mammoth. When he looks at me, my chant dies in my throat. My hands stop tapping on the drum.

Suddenly, I do not feel the strength I once felt, only the ancient terror. . . .

Also by Pat Murphy

The Falling Woman

The Shadow Hunter

Pat Murphy

HEADLINE

Copyright © 1982 by Pat Murphy

First published in Great Britain in 1988
by HEADLINE BOOK PUBLISHING PLC

ISBN 0 7472 3141 9

Printed and bound in Great Britain by
Collins, Glasgow

HEADLINE BOOK PUBLISHING PLC
Headline House
79 Great Titchfield Street
London W1P 7FN

For Richard,
with love

1

I Follow the Bear

1

The shaman of my tribe, a man of power, straddles the shoulder of the fallen mammoth, one leg slung on either shaggy side. The hair on the shaman's legs is as dark and coarse as the hair on the mammoth's side.

I stand at the outer edge of the circle of hunters that surrounds the fallen beast. I am young; I have only ten winters. I stand behind my father and the grass all around us is trampled and bloody from the long battle.

The shaman raises his knife over the throat of the mammoth. The black stone blade glitters in the sun. With a steady hand, he plunges the knife into the throat of the beast. The blood that spills over his hands steams in the cold air and the shaman calls out in a voice of power. He says that the hunt was good, that the beast fought well, that the tribe will waste nothing of the mammoth's body and bone. He calls out to the spirit of the beast.

The mist that rises from the flowing blood swirls in a cloud above the shaman's head. The cloud darkens and forms a shape—the shape of a mammoth standing tall in the bloody grass.

The gray shadow of a mammoth raises his head and stamps his shadow feet and becomes more real, more solid. He glares at the shaman with eyes that glisten like the stone of the blade. The beast shakes his tusks and glares at the hunters who surround him. My father stands between me and the spirit, and his broad shoulders protect me.

The shaman reaches out to the spirit and catches hold of his shadowy trunk. The shaman says in the Old Tongue, the language used to speak to spirits, "You are a good spirit. You will come and be one with my people. You will nourish us and make us strong. We must have your spirit, your strength. . . ."

Does the shaman grow larger in the afternoon sun? Does he grow as the spirit dwindles? I cannot say. The misty spirit changes and flows as the shaman speaks. "You will make us strong," the shaman says, and the spirit becomes more like a shadow or a cloud of mist. The wind puffs through the body and tatters the legs and the spirit is gone. So it always is, after a hunt. The spirit of the hunted beast makes the people strong. So it has always been.

I am young; only ten winters. I have not yet hunted alone and I have not taken a spirit of my own. This day, watching the shaman, I know that I must hunt soon. I must hunt for my own spirit and my true name.

My people make camp by the edge of the meadow. This night, when the moon rises full and round over the meadow, I sleep at my mother's side. And I dream a vision of power.

A shaggy, gray-muzzled she-bear leans over me in this vision. Her great head blocks out the moon. She shakes her head at me and speaks to me in the Old Tongue. "Follow me, little one," she says to me, and she grins. "You are no more than a bite for me, but I need you. Follow me." She is a trickster spirit, this bear. "Follow me," she says and tosses her head as if she is laughing. Her eyes are bright and wise.

I awaken then, just as the full moon is setting. I sit by the coals of the fire and watch the embers flicker. I wait for dawn.

I tell my father what I have dreamed and I tell him that I must hunt to find my name. He nods—yes, it is time for me to hunt alone. I have been a child long enough.

We go to the shaman and he studies me with his dark eyes. The shaman is an old man by the counting of my people; he is nearly forty winters old, and few live through forty winters. He is a wise man with much power. "Was it a true dream?" he asks.

"I could feel her warm breath on my face," I say. "It was true."

"The bear is a strong spirit," he says. "You must be strong as well." And he tells me to go and hunt well.

I will come back with a name and a spirit—or I will not come back. Sometimes, those who go hunting do not return. Sometimes, they do not hunt well and the beasts take their bodies and worry their bones. Sometimes, they hunt well, but they fear the spirit of the beast. Then, the spirit can take the hunter, just as the hunter can take the spirit. The hunter can make the spirit strong, can feed the hazy beast and make it powerful. Then the spirit roams the world, peering out through the eyes of the hunter.

"Do not fear the spirits," my father tells me. "Find a spirit to make you strong."

I take my best spear and my father gives me his stone knife. And he watches me walk away across the meadow, away from the camp of my people. I go to hunt.

I follow the edge of the meadow to the place where a stream crosses the grass. I follow the water away from the meadow, into a ravine where broad-leafed trees shut out the sun. The air smells of dark earth and water and beasts.

On a branch that dangles over the water, I see a strand of gray hair. In the stream, a rock has been shifted—as if by a powerful paw. A cave bear, searching for food after its winter sleep, has passed this way.

I am alert now—awake as my father has taught me to be. I see each mark that the bear's claws have left in the dark earth, each branch that the beast has pushed aside. The scent grows stronger and in a patch of bushes by the side of the stream I see movement.

The bear does not look up from the bushes—with lips and paws, she is plucking berries. Her muzzle is stained red from their juices.

We will be evenly matched, this bear and I. She is young; her head is only a few hand spans higher than my own.

I step closer to her, watching the powerful movements of her paws as she plucks the berries. The bear has an unpredictable spirit. A hunter cannot know what a bear may do. But she has a strong spirit. I would be proud to take the spirit of the bear.

She looks up from the bushes; she looks into my eyes. And I know that she has chosen me, just as I have chosen her. And the air around her becomes suddenly alive—shimmering in the sunlight, just as the air above a fire may suddenly shimmer. She stares at me through the dancing air. And then she is gone. Gone like the spirit of the mammoth.

I step toward the dancing air, careful of the magic it contains, holding my spear ready to meet the bear.

I step into the dancing air.

And the world goes away.

I open my eyes, but a darkness lies over my mind. The world is a shimmering gray, filled with edges.

Edges—I have visited the granite mountains where rocks have fallen in knife-edged sheets as long as I am tall. But the world where I awaken is all edges. Flatness meets flatness in stiff lines.

I cannot move. My arms and legs are stiff and dead. I blink, but I cannot move. The flatness beside me is marked by lines and as I watch, a piece of the flatness shifts.

11

The woman who steps into my room has eyes and skin the color of the sky at night and hair the color of the dark earth. Such a strange woman. She is not like my people, not like my people at all. Her eyes are not protected by brow ridges; her forehead is high and her nose is sharp. She has so little hair on her arms that her skin seems smooth.

A man is with her, but I watch the woman who has such strange, dark skin. In the shimmering gray world of edges, these people move like shadows. What is this world? A place of spirits? A vision of truth? I move now—very slowly, lifting my head to watch these people. When the woman speaks, her voice is soft and her words run together, sounding more like the babbling of water over stone than the language of a people. She speaks to the man and as I listen, I can hear pauses and noises like words in the babble.

She looks at me and points to herself. I catch at the lilting flow of words. What does she want, this woman of the spirit world? With an awkward tongue, I try to repeat some of the sounds. "Amanda," I say. But the sounds are strange and do not feel complete. Again, I say, "Amanda," and I look at her eyes—the color of the sky at night—and I add the word from my language that means darkness. "Amanda—*dark*," I say slowly.

I lift my hand carefully to point to myself and I say my child-name, the name which must serve me until the spirit gives me another. Amanda—*dark* starts to repeat the sounds, tripping and stumbling like a child learning to talk. She stops, starts again, then shakes her head. "Sam," she says, pointing at me. "Sam."

"Sam," I say softly. Is this to be my name? Did the spirit bring me here to give me my new name?

Amanda—*dark* turns to speak to the man who stands beside her and I study his face for the first time. His hair is the color of river mud; his skin is pale. His eyes are restless. My tribe once killed a mother saber-

12

toothed cat near her den and the eyes of this man look like the eyes of her kittens. Shifting and cold. "Roy Morgan," says Amanda—*dark*.

I repeat the sounds, but I do not change this name to improve its sound. This cat-eyed man is not friendly. I do not trust him.

"Sam," says the man. Then in a babble of words, "Sam, the last of the Neanderthals." Then he laughs, a hollow, empty sound like the wind in the mountains. When he laughs, I watch the face of Amanda—*dark* change, closing in on itself, her mouth tightening and her eyes growing darker.

I cannot hold my head up any longer. My eyes close against the shimmering gray world of edges and I sleep.

The air is warm, like the air on a sunny day. I can smell the sweet scent of fruit. I can hear the sound of flowing water.

I open my eyes to the world of edges. The world is white and the darkness is gone from my mind. My body feels stiff, but I can move.

Water flows—from a hole in one flatness to a white bowl. Though the water flows and flows, the bowl does not overflow.

A basket—like the baskets my mother weaves from river reeds—sits on the ground by the flatness marked with lines. The basket is filled with fruit.

I sit up slowly, looking behind me and to each side. All around are the white flatnesses. I keep one flatness to my back as I move to the basket of fruit.

I have never seen fruit like this before. I crouch beside the basket, my back against the flatness. The world is silent, except for the babble of the water and the sound of my breathing.

I eat the sweet fruit and drink of the flowing water and nothing harms me. This world is bounded by four flatnesses and though I push on the flatness where Amanda–*dark* entered, it does not move.

I call out, "Amanda–*dark!*" I hear my own voice, but no answer. "Amanda–*dark!*" Nothing.

I am patient. I will wait to learn why the spirits have brought me to this world of edges. I will wait. I eat, I wash, and I wait. Soon, I sleep again.

I cannot count the times that I sleep and wake. Many times. Sometimes, my sleep is heavy and dreamless and the air carries a strange scent. Then I wake to a new basket of fruit or other strange foods: meat that has been cooked in a fire, vegetables that I have never seen, nuts and grains.

Each time I awaken, I call out to Amanda–*dark* though she never answers. I call out in the Old Tongue to the spirit of the bear. I call out, but no one answers. I wait; I am patient.

But I wonder: has the spirit who brought me to this place forgotten me?

I fast—waiting for guidance. I leave the basket of fruit, nuts and grains. I sleep and I wake and I call out to Amanda–*dark*. I sleep and I wake and I do not eat. I sleep and I wake.

And at last, when I call out to Amanda–*dark*, the flatness marked with lines shifts and Amanda–*dark* is there. She is tall; her dark curly hair is touched with strands of gray. "Hello, Sam," she says, and I recognize the name she has given me: Sam.

"Amanda–*dark*," I say, and I wait without moving.

The gap in the white flatness closes behind her. She looks back quickly and frowns. Then she chooses a round, red fruit from the basket, and holds it out to me. "Apple," she says. "Eat this apple, Sam."

I take the fruit from her hand. "Apple," I say and she nods her head. I choose a yellow fruit from the basket and give it to Amanda–*dark*. "Apple," I say.

She shakes her head, but takes the fruit. "Pear,"

she says. "This is a pear." And she bites the yellow fruit and says, "Eat."

Amanda—*dark* teaches me sounds that are words: apple, pear, orange, banana, water, drink, eat, wall, door, floor. Many words. She laughs when I call the floor a wall, but I learn.

Then she stands and moves toward the flatness that is a door. "Amanda—*dark*," I say, but I do not know how to ask her not to go.

She touches my hand and I know that she will come back. "Good-bye, Sam," she says. She steps through the door and she is gone.

I push against the door after she has gone and it does not move for me. But I am happy. Amanda—*dark* will come back.

Amanda—*dark* comes to me most times that I awaken, and she teaches me words. Language lesson, she calls what she does.

Language lesson: hello, good-bye, yes, no, bread, meat, nut, you, me, sleep, wake. I learn.

She brings me fruit and food and other things and I learn. Language lesson: cup, blanket, pillow, hard, soft, please, thank you. Amanda—*dark* is slow and careful; she uses the words in groups that she calls sentences and I start to understand this babbling language.

Language lesson: over, under, here, there, more, less, now, later, happy, sad, stop, go, going, gone. . . . Yes, I learn. The clock (round white face like the moon) moves its hands (black sticks, but hands are also fingers and palm) to mark the time (time is now, is then, is tomorrow). Sometimes, Amanda—*dark* is sad when she comes in the door, but she laughs when she teaches me.

Amanda—*dark* brings me meat, but the meat has no strength in it. I do not hunt for my food and the meat has no spirit. I try to tell this to Amanda—*dark,* but

15

she does not understand. I do not have the words. And the four walls mark the edges of this world.

"I am going now," she says at the end of each lesson. And at the gap in the flatness (the door in the wall, I know now) she says, "Good-bye, Sam."

And once, I say, right after her, "I am going now?" And when she looks surprised, I add, "Please?"

"No, Sam," she says. "No, you can't go." And I do not have the words to ask her more. At the door, she says, "Good-bye," and her dark eyes are sad.

Amanda—*dark* brings some things that she calls picture books—with bright pictures and dark squiggles that she says are words. Language lesson: friend, touch, hurt, I want, I need, I am . . . you are. So many words and sentences and I can almost talk to Amanda—*dark* about all the important things. Almost.

I am weak from the spiritless meat and fruit. I need to hunt to be strong. I try to tell Amanda—*dark*. I ask her, "Where is the cave bear?" But the words for cave bear are not her words and she does not understand. I draw a picture on a page and point to it. "Where is she?"

"The cave bear," Amanda—*dark* says. "She is out in the valley."

"Out," I say, repeating the simplest of the words. "I need to go out."

"No, Sam," she says. "You can't go out. Roy Morgan wouldn't let you." She hesitates and one dark hand tugs at the fingers of the other. Amanda—*dark* is not happy. "Roy Morgan wouldn't like it if he knew I were here."

"Who is Roy Morgan?" I ask.

"Roy Morgan," she says, and she speaks the name as if it were a word of power. "Roy Morgan started the Project."

I do not understand. "I need to go out," I say, but Amanda—*dark* does not speak. Her face is tired and lined and I wonder how old she is. Old enough to hunt; old enough to have children. "You are my friend, Amanda—*dark*," I say, trying to ease the lines in her face. "You gave me my name. I hunted the bear to find my name."

A few of the lines in her face smooth. "It was my father's name," she says, and I wonder about Amanda—*dark*'s father; perhaps he was a shaman; certainly, a man of power. "What is the name you call me?" she asks.

"Amanda of the darkness," I say. "Your eyes are dark. Like night." When I look in her eyes, I can see the darkness of night and the dire-wolves are howling.

"I still don't understand about the bear and your name," she is saying. "Why were you hunting the bear?"

One of my rough hands grips the other. I fear she will never understand. I do not know the words. "I hunted," I say. "A man who hunts . . ." I hesitate.

"A hunter," she suggests.

"A hunter takes his name from the beast," I say. "The beast gives the name. You must know that."

"Sam, I don't think you understand. I'm no hunter. I've never taken a name from a beast," she says. "I'm just a city kid grown up and working on Roy Morgan's Project and understanding it only part of the time. I'm not a hunter."

Her eyes are dark and now I understand why. She has no name but the name I have given her. No spirit makes her strong. I take her hand in mine. She gave me my name, but she has none of her own.

She will not understand—not just because I cannot find the words, but because she does not have the words. She will never understand.

"You must hunt," I say. "You cannot live on dead meat." But even as I speak, I doubt my words. These people are different; perhaps they do live on dead meat. I long for the day that the spirits will send me home to my own people.

17

I say, "I will be sad to leave you when I go back to my people, Amanda–*dark*. But I will be glad to hunt again."

Her eyes grow darker. "Sam, I don't think ... I thought you knew that. ..." She stops and her eyes are wide and sad. "Your people are gone."

"Gone where?"

"Your people are dead," she says, laying a hand on my shoulder. "Long dead, long gone."

Maybe I do not understand. Where could my tribe have gone? But I think I do understand.

The room is emptier at night after that.

A few days after I had asked about the cave bear, Amanda–*dark* brings a strange woman to see me. This woman's eyes are pale, rimmed with pink, and I can almost see through her skin. When her pale, pink-rimmed eyes look at me, I think that she can see through me.

"Sam, this is Cynthia," Amanda–*dark* says. Her voice is soft and her hands tug at each other. "She works on the Project, too."

"What she means is—I am the other half of the Project," Cynthia says. Her voice is like the falling of snow on ice fields—soft and cold. "Amanda is the past; I am the future."

"She wanted to meet you," Amanda–*dark* begins again.

"Not quite true," the pale woman says. "I said that I would meet him. Not quite the same."

I look to Amanda–*dark,* hoping that she will explain. But Amanda–*dark* is watching the pale woman, her dark eyes wide and her lower lip caught in her teeth.

"Amanda is afraid of me, Sam," the cold woman says in her snowdrift voice. "You see, she knows that I have killed people. No one else knows that for sure."

"Not killed people," Amanda–*dark* mutters. "Not really killed. Just ..."

The woman laughs like icicles falling from a tree to

18

shatter on the frozen ground. "I let my mother drive away when I knew that her car would crash because of her faulty brakes and burn because of a faulty gas tank, and I let her drive away. I was five and I knew, but I did not stop her. I let my father die. I knew that he would, and I could have told him ten years before. He died when I was fifteen, died of a brain tumor that could have been removed—if anyone had known it was there. I knew, and I could have told him, but I didn't. He didn't like me, didn't like me any more than my mother liked me. Neither of them liked me and both of them died." She stands, her hands relaxed at her sides, her face as pale as the white walls. "There were others," she says, and she glances at Amanda–*dark*. "Amanda knows."

"I wouldn't know if I could help it," Amanda–*dark* says. "I don't want to know."

"You don't want to know the past; I don't want to know the future," Cynthia says. "But it makes no difference what we want. Just like it makes no difference what Sam wants. What happens, happens." She looks at me sharply and again I feel clear, transparent as a stream melting from snow. "You will go out, Sam," she says to me. "You'll go out, but you won't like it when you do."

"Don't tell him that," Amanda–*dark* says. Her hands are in fists at her sides. "Don't say . . ."

"I'll say as I please," the pale woman says sharply. "And I'll never tell you if what I say is true. I have a part in your future, Amanda, and in yours, Sam—but I won't tell you what it is." She smiles, watching Amanda–*dark*. "You don't like me, either."

"No," says Amanda–*dark* softly. "I don't like you."

The pale woman turns toward the door. She turns back to say to me, "I'll see you again, Sam." Then she steps through the door and Amanda–*dark* follows.

Amanda–*dark* returns alone.

19

"She said that I would go out," I say to Amanda–*dark*. "When will I go?"

Amanda–*dark* looks sad and puzzled and rubs one of her long-fingered hands with the other. "You can't go out, Sam. Roy Morgan would ..." She stops. "I shouldn't even be here. Roy Morgan wouldn't like it. But I had to. I felt responsible for you." She stops at the word that I do not know.

"Why?" I ask, wanting her to keep talking, keep explaining so that I will understand a few words. Just a few words I can think about in the night and try to understand.

"I brought you here," she says. "You got in the way of the field. Roy Morgan wanted the bear. You must have rushed into the field right after I focused on the bear." She shakes her head. "Why did you do that? You ended up on the floor of the reception chamber, knocked out by the tranquilizer we had gassed in for the bear. And I ended up responsible for you." She is shaking her head. "I brought you here."

She does not say good-bye; she leaves without looking back and I do not try to stop her.

That night, I lie awake and think about Amanda–*dark* and the words she has said. Roy Morgan would not like me to go out, but what does Roy Morgan matter? And she brought me here; Amanda–*dark* brought me. I am puzzled. Who brought me—Amanda–*dark* or the she-bear spirit?

The next day, Amanda–*dark* does not come. I eat from the basket of fruit and wonder when she will come again.

After three days, she comes, and still her eyes are dark and sad when she looks at me. "Amanda–*dark*," I say. "I am glad you are here."

"Come on, Sam," she says. "You come with me. Cynthia said you'd go out and you will." She takes my hand in her warm, dark hand and leads me through the door.

I follow Amanda—*dark* through long, white rooms. . . . ("Corridors," she tells me. "Or else, hallways." I am still learning.) Through hallways, then. I follow her, and she talks, using words I do not know. "It's a holiday," she says. "Just a skeleton crew. Roy Morgan . . ." She hesitates. "Roy Morgan gave everyone a day off. Cynthia's still here. She and I are always here. We've really got nowhere else to go."

She takes me through another door into a room where a dire-wolf lies on the floor behind a wire wall. The dire-wolf looks up and I stop in the doorway. "It's all right," Amanda—*dark* says. "He's tame. Besides, he's in a cage."

I have seen dire-wolves pull down the camels of the plains, ripping at the grazers' legs and dodging kicks. I have heard the packs howling in the darkness, as if they waited just beyond the fire's rim. I see the moonlight of forgotten nights in this beast's eyes and I stop in the doorway.

"This is Lobo," Amanda—*dark* says. She reaches through the wire to scratch the beast's head. "He was the first I brought back." The animal whines deep in his throat and moonlit memories fade from his eyes. It is not a wolf now, but some other animal she pets. The light in its eyes is a mad one—a blend of moonlight and the glow of the lights in the room.

"He's a good wolf, aren't you, Lobo?" Amanda—*dark* says.

"Not good," I say, and Amanda—*dark* watches me, studying my face. "It is . . ." I hesitate. I do not have the words to name the light that has entered the dire-wolf's eyes. Some tomorrow, some future time, I know that Amanda—*dark* will reach down to scratch the beast's ears and his past will rise up and Lobo will meet her hand with his teeth. Unable to finish, I shrug.

Amanda—*dark* frowns without understanding. She turns away from the wolf and touches a switch and does things that I do not know how to describe on a part of the wall that has many clock faces, though they do not seem to tell the time.

A part of the wall has come alive with colors that move. Amanda–*dark* points to the moving colors. "I wanted you to see this, Sam," she says. "This is Roy Morgan's world."

As I look, I see shapes in the colored lines. I see a hazy view of a world I know.

The dark spots on the green fields are camels and swine, grazing on the tall grass of the valley floor. I can see a small stream snaking around the edge of the meadow. Behind the beasts, a great rocky slope rises into mountains. This is a rich valley, one that could support a large tribe. I am looking down, as if from a mountain.

"This is the world that Roy Morgan is building," Amanda–*dark* says. "This is the Project. You're a part of it and I'm a part of it."

"Where are the people?" I ask.

Amanda–*dark* frowns. "You're the only person who belongs in this world of Roy Morgan's. The only one."

She touches the switch and the picture of the valley goes away, leaving a gray patch of wall in a world with edges. Amanda–*dark* takes my hand and leads me to another door.

And the wind from beyond the door carries strange scents and echoing sounds. She steps through the door and I follow.

I have stood on the edge of a mountain chasm. I stood by my father and tossed a rock into the space. The rock fell and bounced from the walls of the canyon, fell and bounced, carrying its echoes with it, fell and bounced until I could no longer hear it, but I knew that far below, the rock still fell. I have stood on the edge of a chasm where the wind carried the echoes of the river that flowed far below.

Amanda—*dark* and I stand on a gray walkway. The ceiling vaults high above us. Below us, no river flows.

I have no words to say what lies beneath us. Words bounce away from this place, as a rock bounces from the walls of a canyon, and I can only hear the echoes. This place is a gray canyon filled with shadows and echoes.

Amanda—*dark* grips the cold, metal bar that separates us from the canyon—room. Her teeth have caught her lower lip; her eyes dart here and there, studying the shadows. A man who owns a fine stone knife might look at it so; a woman with a child may have that look when she lifts it to suck.

"This is what brought you here, Sam," she says.

"You brought me here, Amanda—*dark*," I say. She gave me my name. She and the bear led me to this place.

"I am part of this," she says. "Just a part. Roy Morgan built it. He used his father's money and his own imagination." She stops for a moment then. "He isn't a bad man, Sam. He really isn't. He has big dreams and big fears. He makes rules because he is afraid. Sometimes, I think he is afraid of me."

Amanda—*dark* has a strong spirit; sometimes I can see it in her eyes. Roy Morgan does well to fear her.

"That's my post," she says. She points to a shadowy corner and I peer toward it. "I focus the machine," she says. "Before I came, they never knew what they would bring back from the past. A clump of dirt, a rock, nothing at all. Then Roy Morgan found a skinny black teenager who had a strange talent. She didn't see the future, not this one. She saw the past, sort of. Hold up a card and she could tell you what card you held up last week. Take her to an old house and she could tell you about the family that lived there a hundred years ago. Or about the Indians that used to camp on the same spot. She knew things that she shouldn't about people and places, mostly long dead.

Not a very useful talent—unless you're into blackmail, and when you're weak and black and a woman, blackmail isn't the smartest thing to try." Her hands are gripping the railing. "Not a very useful talent, but Roy Morgan found a use for me. He needed someone to focus on what used to be." She keeps looking toward the shadowy corner that is her post. "And now he's found another one he can use."

"Cynthia," I say.

She continues as if she has not heard me. "Cynthia sees the future and Roy Morgan is experimenting with throwing things into the future. I don't like that. I don't like the future. It scares me."

I am watching the floor of the canyon-room and I see a movement. A woman in a white coat. I point to her just as she looks up at us. It is Cynthia, and her eyes are filled with knowledge of the time ahead.

"I'll be here, Amanda," Cynthia calls up to us. Her words are thin, distorted by echoes. "When you need me, I'm here."

Amanda—*dark* frowns.

"What does she mean?" I ask. "Why would you need her?"

Amanda—*dark* watches Cynthia move away into the shadows. "She says that I will need her soon. She says that today I will come running to her for help." Amanda—*dark* shakes her head. "I don't need her. I don't even like her." She shakes her head again and turns to me. "Do you understand all that I have been telling you, Sam? I never know how much you understand."

"Some," I say. "Not all."

"You're my friend, Sam. I'm sorry I brought you here, but at the same time, I'm glad. I don't have many friends," she says. She takes my hand in hers.

"We are friends," I say.

She hesitates. "I don't know what I can do for you, Sam. I can't send you home."

"Take me out," I say. I wave my hand at the flat walls and the hard corners all around us. "Take me to hunt. I need to hunt."

She shakes her head quickly, frowning. Then she squeezes my hand gently. "I will try. I don't know what I can do, but I will try."

I follow her back along the corridor from which we have come.

My room is dark when we step through the door, and the air holds a different scent. I stand between Amanda–*dark* and the strange scent. Amanda–*dark* switches on the light, and I stand between her and Roy Morgan. Roy Morgan is smiling; his eyes are cold. "Hello, Amanda," he says.

My back is to Amanda–*dark*. I cannot see her face. But her voice is thin and tense. "Hello. I didn't think. . . ." Her voice trails off into silence.

Not quite silence. I can hear Amanda–*dark* breathing. I am tense, ready—as if for a hunt.

"You've been watching me," she says softly.

"I'm always watching. Surely you didn't think you were fooling me," Roy Morgan says. "I've been following Sam's progress with great interest. I decided to let the language lessons continue, but now that you want to try to help him out, plan some great escape, maybe . . ."

"I didn't think it mattered to you," she says. I want to turn around to comfort her, but I must face the danger. I must face Roy Morgan.

"It mattered that you were breaking the rules," he says. His voice is harsh. "You were breaking my rules and that matters very much. Of course, I'll have to take you off the Project now. You will have to leave."

I hear Amanda–*dark* breathe in sharply and I know that Roy Morgan hears her because he stops talking. I think of Amanda–*dark*'s face when she was looking down at the Project. She belongs here. She said that she had nowhere else to go.

25

Roy Morgan is smiling. "You didn't think you were indispensable, did you? No one is indispensable."

"How can you run the Project without me?"

"The focus is changing," he says. "I am looking forward now, not back. We have what we wanted from the past."

"You're trying to scare me," she says. "You can't do without me."

"You have it wrong," he says. "No one else has the money or the desire to build a facility like this one. You'll never be able to duplicate this, and you'll never find a place to use your talent again." His smile broadens. "But you'll have to try."

I hear Amanda—*dark*'s breath come and go quickly. "You came alone."

"Why not? You wouldn't hurt me, since someday I might relent."

"Sam," she says suddenly. I tense, ready to attack this smiling man. "Just keep him here. Don't let him follow me."

I hear the door open and close behind me. Roy Morgan takes a step toward it, and I step to block his path. "You are not going," I say, and my voice is a growl.

"Now, Sam," he says. "Amanda can't go anywhere anyway." He waits a moment, but I do not move. He takes a step back. "And she won't be back. You can be sure of that. I don't know where she thinks she's running to."

I know where she is running. She is running to where Cynthia waits by the machine that can throw things into the future. She is running to the shadowy cavern that is the Project, seeking help from the woman she does not like.

"Cynthia warned me that I'd have to watch her," Roy Morgan says. "She said Amanda could not be trusted. She was right."

Amanda—*dark* is running to an enemy for help and

I can do nothing to stop her. I stand between Roy Morgan and the door.

"So she trained you to be a bodyguard," he says. He is watching the door.

I do not know the last word, but I do not like the way he says it. "I am Amanda–*dark*'s friend," I say. "She will be back."

He laughs, shaking his head. I do not like the sound of his laugh. It reminds me of the howling of wolves outside the circle of firelight. "You're a loyal friend," he says, "but maybe a foolish one."

I stand between him and the door and I watch the clock mark the passage of ten minutes, twenty minutes, half an hour. I do not speak to Roy Morgan. Roy Morgan speaks to me, but I do not reply. I am thinking of Amanda–*dark*. I am wondering when I will see her again. "I think we're stalemated, Sam," Roy Morgan says. "You might as well let me leave. Amanda's gone."

I shake my head and I wait. Another half hour passes. Still, I watch Roy Morgan.

There is a strange scent in the air. I feel very tired and my eyes begin to close. Roy Morgan is sitting on the floor, leaning against the wall. "Security guard finally checked in on this room," he says sleepily. "Took long enough."

My eyes close. I sit on the floor slowly and I sleep. When I awaken, Roy Morgan is gone. When I push against the door, it does not open.

I sit on the pillows and wait for Amanda–*dark* to return.

I eat the fruit that is left by the door. I drink the water. I sleep and I wait.

On the third day, the heavy scent stings my nose again. I lean against the white wall and I close my eyes. I will sleep for a time, just a short time. I sleep.

2

I awaken in a world without walls. I lie atop a small rock outcropping at one edge of a wide, grassy valley. The valley is ringed with tall mountains of gray stone.

I recognize the profile of the mountains from the strange picture that Amanda—*dark* showed me, and I realize that the walls are still around me. I cannot see them, but I know they are there because I am still in Roy Morgan's world.

This place is warmer than the valley where my tribe lives. The grass is taller than the grass of our valley. The wind is warm, not like the wind off the ice fields that always carried the scent of winter. I do not trust this warm, sweet-scented world.

Across the valley, I see grazing animals—deer, I think, but they are not the kind of deer my people hunt. These are smaller; their fur is lighter in color. Still, they are deer, beasts that I can hunt.

I hear a sound in the tall grass beneath my ledge, a coughing, growling sound. I lean over the edge to look below. A lone hyena stands at the edge of the tall grass. She steps out onto the barren ground, and I see a pup following her. Still awkward, the pup tries to trot, but its feet tangle and its gait is clumsy. The bitch hyena is alert—ears up, head held high. She looks suddenly in my direction and I wonder what small sound I have made. I am dull from my days in

28

the room, from days of the same sights and scents and sounds. Only as the hyena and her pup fade back into the tall grass do I find their scent on the wind.

I have been too long out of the wind. I have been too long away from the beasts and the sky.

The sun rises and sets and rises and sets and rises and sets. I do not count the days. I am alone.

I find fruit on the trees at the edge of the valley. Some is familiar—like fruit my tribe eats; some looks like the fruit Amanda—*dark* brought me. I eat fruit and explore the valley. I find shelter beneath an overhang near the rock face where I awakened. I drink clear water from a spring that is hidden in the trees.

Most important, I prepare for the hunt. I find an outcropping of the hard flint that my tribe uses for ax heads and I make a hand ax. I find a grove of the trees that we use to make spears and I use my ax to cut several spears. I sharpen them with a knifelike sliver chipped from the flint. I harden the spearpoints in the fire.

With my sharpened spears, I creep through the grass toward a grazing herd of deer. I have been watching them for several days—one old buck always grazes a short distance from the others, always a little apart.

I crawl through the grass slowly, carefully. The sun moves from near the horizon to a point overhead, and still I crawl. I am hunting and I am a part of the meadow. The sound of my breath is just the humming of an insect; the sound when my arm brushes a grass stalk is the rustle of the wind. I am part of the meadow.

The buck is grazing near the tall grass where I lie. I am tense, ready. I am a part of the tall grass, part of the meadow, part of the buck before me. The hunt is upon me.

Does the wind shift, playing with the grass tops? The buck looks up, wide-eyed, and I leap from my hiding place. The herd is scattering, but already I am flinging the sharp-tipped spear at the old buck, and I call out words in the Old Tongue of my people. I ask the spirit of the buck to accept death. The spear pierces the smooth brown fur and the eyes of the buck widen still farther. He snorts and begins running through the tall grass, following his herd. I run after him and the air is hot with the scent of blood.

Twice more, I fling spears at him. One strikes, one fails. The two spears dangle from his side as he trots—head high, eyes wide, his breast flecked with the foam from his nostrils. He runs and I run after him.

The sun is setting over the mountains. I have chased the buck across the valley. He has faltered, almost stumbled three times, but each time he has recovered to keep on running, just out of my reach. His spirit is strong.

At last, I find him in a darkening grove of trees. His head hangs low. He does not look up when I come near. Again, I ask him for his spirit, then I cast my last spear.

He staggers with the impact, and falls to his knees. He tries to recover, then collapses to lie on the ground. Still, his eyes are open. Still, his breath comes quick in his throat.

I gently cut his throat with my flint blade and the blood spills out over my hands. I call in the Old Tongue to his spirit. His spirit can make me strong, though it will never be my spirit. My spirit is the bear spirit that brought me here; the spirit that found me my name. But the buck can make me strong.

The spirit rises with a frightening speed. No old buck, this spirit. The spread of his antlers is as wide as I am tall. His stance is that of a buck in his prime. He snorts and tosses his head—shaking his antlers and stamping a hoof against the ground. Soundlessly.

I speak softly in the Old Tongue, speaking his praise. The wide brown eyes focus on me. This spirit has no fear. The spirit knows me for the one who set it free.

His nostrils widen at the scent of me and he rears up to tower above me, hooves kicking against the air.

I fear this wild spirit—fear it as I have never feared a living beast. I remember the mammoth spirit and remember how my father stood between me and the spirit. I wish that my father were with me. I wish I had my tribe around me. I feel weak and tired.

I step back and the spirit grows taller, vast and gray against the setting sun. The spirit tosses its proud horns in the dying light.

Sunset, I think, and I feel as if the light could shine through me. I have no power in me. Amanda—*dark* is gone; my people are gone. And the eyes of the buck are bright with power. I have not the strength I had when first I left my tribe.

I raise my knife against the spirit, as I would against a living beast. I step back, but as I step I catch the scent of blood in the air. The body of the buck lies at my feet—beneath the stamping feet of the spirit.

I remember the feel of the grass whipping against my legs when I chased the buck down. I remember the sound of my first spear striking. I remember that my name is Sam and my spirit is the bear spirit. I remember that I killed the beast. I am strong.

I look into the eyes of the buck spirit and I say, in the Old Tongue, "You will make me strong, powerful one." And I put my knife at my side and hold my hand out to the beast. I close my eyes and I feel the spirit in me—large and strong and wild. I welcome the spirit.

I remember the taste of buds in the spring, the feel of snow around my haunches in the winter, the pounding of my heart when I ran from a saber-toothed cat and the weight of antlers upon my head. And somewhere, I can hear hooves drumming like the rain on the grass and I remember my herd running and myself running with them. I am running; I am free; I am strong.

"You will make me strong," I mutter in the Old

Tongue. I hear the leaves rustling above my head and I feel the wind on my shoulders. "The hunt was good," I say.

I open my eyes to the world. I am strong and the buck is a part of me. With my flint blade, I tear at the buck's hide and think of how I will scrape and cure the skin to use as a blanket this winter. I hear a sound and catch a strange scent on the wind. I look up, as alert as the buck was in his prime.

Roy Morgan watches me from the shadow at the edge of the clearing.

I stand, still holding the bloody blade. Why has he followed me here?

"Hello, Sam," he says. He waits for a moment, and I do not move. "That was an impressive hunt."

Still, I do not move and I do not speak. The silence stretches before him like his shadow in the setting sun and he shifts his feet uneasily. "I thought you might have decided that we can be friends now. Can we be friends?"

I hear the hollowness in his voice. Like the echoes in the gray canyon-room. Amanda—*dark* had said that he was not a bad man. He was a man with big ideas and big fears. But not a bad man.

Roy Morgan waits, but I do not speak. He looks down at the buck, at the blood on the forest floor and the insects that buzz around my head. "I watched you hunt this deer," he says. "We have easier ways of killing. I'll show you how to kill from a distance." He frowns down at the buck. "Why did you slit its throat?" he asks. "It was already dead."

He does not understand the ways of the spirit. Amanda—*dark* did not understand me when I tried to explain the power of the spirit to her. I would not try to explain to this empty man.

"Where is Amanda—*dark?*" I ask him suddenly.

He hesitates. "She's gone away."

"Where?"

"I don't know," he says and that tells me enough. He did not catch her. Though I do not know why she ran or what would have happened if she had not, I was very glad he did not catch her. "You would be better off forgetting about Amanda."

"She is my friend," I say.

"I will be your friend."

"How?" I ask. "How do you wish to be my friend?"

"Let me hunt with you," he says. "I want . . ." His voice is hollow and empty. "I want to hunt. This is my world, but . . ." He looks at the dead buck, at the trees, at the meadow and the faraway herd of deer. "My world, but I don't, I can't. . . ." He stops. When he speaks again, the hollowness in his voice is hidden beneath a hardness, brittle like new ice. "This world doesn't know it's mine."

"This is the world of the beasts," I say.

He shakes his head and says, "I'll hunt the beasts and they'll know it's my world."

"No," I say. "It is the world of the beasts."

He has no spirit. He is hollow, empty. I do not understand him. As I watch, his face is changing, becoming harder, more brittle.

"Take me hunting, Sam. Take me, or I will go alone and you'll be put back in the room with four white walls and you can wait there for your friend Amanda. You'll wait for a long time."

I watch his face. I have my knife. I can kill this man who does not understand the world he has made. Or I can take him hunting. And the beasts will decide what happens. This world of his will decide.

I nod. "I will take you hunting. Tomorrow. Then, we will hunt."

"Tomorrow," he says. He leaves me then, moving away in the fading light to a destination that I do not understand. I do not want to understand.

I take the meat and the hide of the buck to a tree that is a short run from my shelter. I carry it on my back and three times I run from the forest to my tree, carrying the warm and heavy meat. The third time, I must drive a cave hyena from the buck. But I am strong and this beast is a coward. I shout in the Old Tongue and toss a sharp-edged rock to strike her on the flank. I leave her a piece of haunch and she does not follow. The hyena is a coward and a traitor. Mean and treacherous.

I sleep in my shelter, some distance from the meat. In the night, I awaken to tend the fire and I listen to the sounds of the world: grunting, coughing, roaring with beasts. Roy Morgan does not know this world; he carries the scent of the gray canyon-room with him and he does not know the beasts. But I am strong with the spirit of the buck.

I awaken to the thin light of dawn and the sound of sly footsteps in the grass. I smell Roy Morgan before I see him—a scent of smoke and sweat. I tense and put a hand on my knife, but I lie still, as if asleep.

Roy Morgan carries a stick that glitters in the sun. He stops a few paces from me, raises the stick to his shoulder, and points it at a flock of birds feeding in the grass.

The sound is like thunder and my hand clenches my knife. The flock rises in flight, but one bird lies in the grass. The reek of bitter smoke touches me.

Roy Morgan looks back to find me watching him. "This is a rifle. It kills at a distance." I stand, my knife still in my hand. "Here, hold it," Roy Morgan says, holding the stick out to me.

I hold the rifle in my hand, as Roy Morgan has carried it. I do not like this rifle.

"I'll teach you to use it," Roy Morgan says.

"No," I say. "It is not good." The rifle is bright and warm to the touch. But the bird died with no warning. It is not good. It smells wrong. I will not use this rifle on the hunt.

"It isn't difficult," he says. "When we hunt, you . . ."

"I will use my spear," I say.

"Maybe I was wrong when I figured you were smart, Sam," he says. Then his eyes narrow. "I wondered why it was that your tribe died off like it did. I guess maybe we humans were better at some things. Like learning new ways of killing." His voice is hollow and weary. He starts to reach out, and for a moment I think he may touch my shoulder like a friend.

In that moment, I begin to explain, "You must be close to the beast," I say. "To be strong in the hunt, you must take the spirit of the beast. With this rifle you take the beast, but not the spirit." I tried to think as a shaman would think, of how the rifle could be used. "I do not know. . . ."

Roy Morgan takes the rifle from my hands. "Whatever you say, you have to admit that a spear is no match for this. This could stop a bear in its tracks."

He fears the beasts. As he fears this world he made, as he feared Amanda—*dark,* as he fears me. He fears the beasts.

"No match for this rifle at all," he says and his empty eyes study me in the dawn light. "What shall we hunt?"

I hesitate. "The beast to be hunted will choose us," I say. "We do not choose."

"What do you mean, it'll choose us?" He starts. "If this is my hunt . . ."

I shrug, silently. "We will see."

I start walking toward the tree where the meat has hung this night. By the tree there will be tracks of the grunting, coughing, roaring beasts of the night. Roy Morgan follows, silent now except for his boots tramping in the grass.

I catch a scent on the wind and I look in the direction of the tree where the meat hangs. The cave hyena stands in the grass. The morning light has touched her spotted coat with gold and the dew from the grass glistens on the fur of her haunches. Her eyes are mean, but she is a strong beast with powerful shoulders and a wicked face.

"There," says Roy Morgan. "An easy shot."

Startled by the movement, the beast lifts her head higher to sample the wind. The spirit has chosen Roy Morgan; he has chosen the spirit.

"Wait," I say. "This beast is a coward, her spirit is . . ."

The sound of the rifle is like thunder in the mountains; the scent is as bitter as the smoke of the shaman's fire when he is calling the spirits.

The beast falls heavily. Faraway birds rise from the meadow, fleeing the sound of the rifle. The hyena lies still.

"It is not good," I say to the world around me. "Not good."

"His head'll be a trophy," Roy Morgan laughs. "His fur will be a rug." He runs to where the beast lies in the grass and I let him run. I stand in the thin sunshine and watch the birds fly over the valley. I see Roy Morgan kneel by the hyena and his metal knife flashes in the sun.

Is it fog that rises from the body of the beast? Is it a shadow in the shape of a hyena that towers above the kneeling man? The sun is blocked by a passing cloud and the shadow is gone.

I walk slowly across the meadow toward the man.

Roy Morgan's hands are red with the blood of the beast. His rifle is on the ground beside him; his knife is in his hands.

He stands to meet me, but still he looks at the hyena on the ground. "A fine trophy," he says, but his voice is a little weak, a little puzzled. He does not understand. "You know, Sam, Cynthia said that I would regret coming to this valley. She said that evil waited for me here and she laughed." He looks down at the beast and rubs at the blood on one hand with his other hand. "I thought you might try to kill me because Amanda had gone away. But I didn't really think you'd do that. That's not the way you operate. You're not as mean as we humans are." He raises his eyes to look at me.

In his eyes, there is the spirit of the hyena—craven and fearful. The hyena has him and he cowers with the beast. Not a noble spirit. A spirit that saps his strength and makes him afraid of shadows.

"You did not try to kill me," he says.

I will never need to kill him. He has found his own fate.

"This is my world," he says.

I nod, knowing that now he is right. This is a world of the beasts.

3

Roy Morgan took the hyena's head and hide and left her carcass. It lies far from the place I sleep, but I can smell the beast's blood on the wind. The moon is full and I am alone.

I hear insects in the grass; I hear the faraway scream of a saber-toothed cat. And I hear a quiet whimpering on the wind.

The hyena bitch had a pup.

The hyena is a mean and cowardly beast. Her spirit is weak and selfish. When she hunts, she hunts the weakest animals. And the hyena's laughter in the night is a wicked sound.

But the pup cries by the carcass of his mother.

I take a strip of meat from the carcass of the buck I killed. I go to the place where the pup is crying. The beast's eyes glow gold in the light of the full moon.

"We are brothers of a sort," I say to the pup. He watches me silently. My tribe is gone; my world is gone; Amanda—*dark* is gone. "Take this," I say. I toss him the meat and he backs away, his ears back and his hindquarters flattened to the ground. When I step back, he sniffs at the meat. I think of Amanda—*dark* and the dire-wolf she called Lobo. The beast was her friend—a kind of friend. But that was her way, not mine.

"Take the meat and go," I say to the pup. "Hunt your own food, find your own way. Do not confuse this world with another."

He drags the meat away from me, into the bushes.

I go back to the overhanging rock and I sleep, listening to the insects sing in the meadow.

The morning is clear and cold. The wind of the night has carried away the scent of Roy Morgan's rifle and his tobacco. Roy Morgan is gone and this valley is mine.

I explore my Valley and I learn its ways. The overhanging rock shelters me each night. I learn more about the beasts that graze in the meadow: the red deer, the bison, the giant elk with antlers as wide as I am tall. The ravens of this world are the same as the ravens of my world, but the squirrels and mice and small birds are different. Some of the plants are the same; some are new to me. I learn.

The stream runs along one edge of the Valley, spreading to make a low, marshy area at the mountain's feet. Sweet, green plants grow here and I gather herbs that I remember the shaman using. Small, shy deer live in the brush of the swamp. I see a new beast—like a mammoth, only less shaggy and taller, with straight tusks rather than curved. I learn where the rabbits feed, where berries grow and where there are roots to gather. At night, I hear wolves and saber-toothed cats. I see signs of wild cats and brown bears by the stream.

I climb the cold stone slopes that rise from the Valley floor. The mountains' sides are weathered and old. Snow and ice have cut crevices in the rock, and low bushes cling in the cracks. In places, the rock has shattered, leaving a jumble of pieces ready to tumble away down the mountain. A small stream flows over the rocks, fed by a spring perhaps. I climb in the mountains, but I never climb to the source of the stream.

Though the wind is still warm, I prepare for winter. I scrape the buck's hide and work it until it is soft and I can wrap it around me when I sleep. The overhang that protects me now will not keep out the snow, so I build a hut after the way of my tribe. Sturdy branches set in a circle and held in place with rocks form a dome; I cover it with leaves and grass and bark. When the snow comes, it will cover the grass and bark and make a second wall to keep out the wind.

I make loops from the sinew of the buck and set them where they will catch rabbits. I kill another deer—a doe without a fawn. With her hide and the sinew of her legs, I sew moccasins and leggings. With rabbit skins, I make a tunic for when the days grow cold.

It is hard to work alone, always alone. I think of my tribe, getting ready for winter in the real world. They will have moved since I left to hunt the bear—perhaps to the winter camp by now. I wonder when I will return to them.

And I think about hunting the bear who brought me here.

One day, I find by the stream the tracks of a young cave bear, younger than the one I followed to this place. I follow the trail until I lose it on the slope of the mountain.

Another day, higher on the mountain, I find a place where an older bear has been tearing up moss and digging for roots. I recognize the look of the track—this is the she-bear who led me here.

Fall is the wrong time to hunt the bear. She is strong and alert now. I will wait until winter, when the bear has made her den and she sleeps.

But I follow her tracks to find her den. A narrow path leads to a low, broad cave mouth that opens into darkness. The small ledge in front of the cave ends in a sheer drop; jagged rocks lie below. The rock of the ledge has been scraped by her claws; the air holds her scent. I know, by the look of the tracks and the droppings, that the cave is empty now. But I will hunt here in winter, when the snow is on the ground and the she-bear sleeps.

From the ledge before the cave, I look out over the Valley. This is the highest I have climbed on these slopes. The top of the ridge that surrounds the Valley is not far above me.

Below, I can see dark spots that are deer grazing in the meadow. A mammoth moves along the edge of the grass, in and out of the trees. This is a rich Valley, a good place to live. I know that Amanda—*dark* will come back and when she does, I will be waiting for her in this rich world. Beyond the meadow, the rocky slope rises into the mountains.

I frown, remembering when I stood with Amanda—*dark* and watched a screen that showed this world. The rocks rose beyond the meadow just like this; the stream was just so; the woods were as I see them now.

The sound that I hear behind me does not belong in my Valley. A small click—like the sound the clock in my room made when its hand moved to mark the passage of a minute.

I look back to the cave mouth. Above the mouth, on

the rocky slope, in the darkness of a crack in the rock, I can see a circle—like an eye looking out of the darkness. I hear another click—like the click of a mouse's claw against a nut. I do not know what hides in this crack, but I know that it does not belong in my Valley. This is not my Valley while Roy Morgan watches from a crack in the rock.

I scramble up the steep slope, clinging to the rough rock with both hands. There is a narrow ledge above the cave mouth, where I stand while I pull on the cold metal box that hides in the darkness. I cannot move it. With a rock, I try to break the glass of the eye, hammering awkwardly within the crack. I scrape my hands against the rock, but the eye does not break.

From the ledge below, I carry rocks and sand and I fill the crack, walling the eye in, blocking it off. I slide back to the ledge by the cave of the bear and I look up. There is no crack now, just a mass of rock and sand. I rub my hands together to brush off the dirt and I grin. Roy Morgan built this world, but I live here now.

The sun shines overhead. I am nearly to the top of the ridge. It is a good day, a warm day, so I follow the narrow trail away from the bear's cave and I take winding paths that lead toward the top of the ridge. I want to see my Valley from the highest point.

Around me, gray boulders stand. When I walk between them, the air is cool and it smells of water and darkness. When I walk in the sunshine, the air smells of grass and pine and warmth.

A fox trots ahead of me. He is not hunting, but he moves with a purpose. His ears are up and his head is held high. He has the look of a beast on his way to an easy kill. I follow him.

Pines grow here, trees that have been dwarfed by the winds and winter snows. The fox moves through the trees, not stopping to chase the squirrels that run before him.

At the top of the ridge, the fox stops beside a gray

rock that points to the sky like a sharp tooth. A smooth rock, as tall as I am. A step away from this rock, there is another rock that is just as tall and smooth. I look along the ridge and in the distance I see another pair of the gray rock teeth.

The fox sits by the tooth and looks up, as if he expects food to fall from the sky. I wait, watching him.

Birds sing in the pines. They fly over my head, dipping and swooping. The fox watches them. Two fly from the tree near me toward a tree beyond the gray teeth. One is chasing the other as they draw even with the gray teeth.

And they fall.

The first bird strikes hard. Though I can see the trees beyond, the bird drops as if it had struck a cliff. The second begins to swerve and strikes the cliff that is not there. The fox grabs the first before it hits the ground and pounces on the second soon after.

The fox is fat and well fed.

The wind that blows against my skin is suddenly cooler. I go to the gray teeth. The fox trots away from me, to the next pair of teeth, where he will wait for birds to fall from the sky. I lay my hand against the gray tooth. It is smooth metal. Like the glistening eye, it does not belong in my Valley. I can feel a hum within the metal—a stirring as if the gray tooth were alive. I lay my ear against it and listen to the hum inside.

I push my hand between the two teeth. The air between them is cold and still. Then I hit a barrier—the same wall that stopped the bird. A hard, cold wall like a sheet of ice. It does not yield when I push against it. I walk to one side of the tooth and I find the same barrier.

The deer trail that the fox followed leads to the teeth and no further. Roy Morgan has put walls around his world and I am inside them.

I go back to the Valley that I call my own. Finding

the eye and the barrier does not change this Valley that is my world, but I watch more carefully for things that do not belong here.

I find another eye, hidden in the rocks by the spring. I had never heard it click because the babbling of the water covered its sounds. I find an eye in the marsh, another on the low rocky slopes at the far end of the Valley, another in the pine forest beside the marsh. Each time, I bury the eye, break it, block its view of my world. After a time, I find no more.

I have a store of dried meat, roots, berries, and nuts in my hut. I am ready for winter and I wait for the snow to fall. When the snow is deep and the days are as cold as the nights, when the wind is fierce, it will be time to hunt the bear. I wait.

The third snowfall of winter has covered the meadow. I walk beside the stream, my moccasins warm on my feet. I go to see if my traps have caught any rabbits.

But a scream cuts through the mountains. Not the scream of a cat, not the scream of a man—but a long, hoarse cry, like a chant all on one note, like the wail of a bull mammoth. But this scream goes on and on.

I crouch in the bushes beside the meadow, motionless in the shadows.

The wind carries the scent of bitter smoke. And the scream is louder—like a mountain crying out in protest.

A strange beast runs over the clean snow. The mountains echo with its screaming. A bundled figure—could a person ride this wailing beast?—clings to its back.

The beast stops by my hut. The scream stops. I wait and I watch. The person—it is a person—steps from the back of the beast. By the flat rock beside the hut, she throws back the hood of her cloak.

I see her silvery hair and I know her—Cynthia of the frozen eyes. She is looking at me, across the meadow. She knows that I am here.

I do not cross the trail of the strange beast as I walk toward her. I do not want my tracks to mingle with those strange tracks that stretch over the mountain and beyond the Barrier.

Cynthia is smiling. Her breath makes steam in the air. I stop several paces from her and her beast. I look at her and study her pale eyes. She waits. "Where is Amanda—*dark*?" I ask at last.

Still, she smiles. "You can come closer, Sam," she says. "This isn't an animal. It's a snowmobile. It won't hurt you."

I do not fear the snowmobile—it is quiet and motionless. But I do not step nearer. "Where is Amanda—*dark*?" I ask again.

"You're asking the wrong question, Sam," Cynthia says. "You should ask, 'When is Amanda—*dark*?'"

Her words make no sense to me. "When?" I repeat.

"She came to me for help and I said that the only way I could help was to send her forward, throw her forward to another time. And she went."

I do not understand all this. "Why did she go?"

Cynthia's breath makes small puffs of steam when she laughs. "She wanted to help you, Sam. I told her that was the only way she'd be able to help. So she went." Her laughter has an edge that I do not like. Like the brittle edge of broken ice, which can cut you before you feel the pain.

"Why did you send her away?" I ask.

"She was in my way, and she isn't now." Cynthia is smiling. "Do you want to know the future I see? You're not important in this future. Amanda—*dark*'s not important. But I am important and powerful. Roy Morgan relies on me and trusts me."

I shake my head with impatience. I do not care about the power she seeks. I start to turn away.

"Wait," she says. "You have questions for me."

I stop. I have questions. When will I go back to my

own people? What must I do to leave this spirit world behind? If I hunt the bear, is that enough?

"Roy Morgan will be coming back in the spring," she says. "You'll be here to meet him."

I shake my head. If I hunt the bear and return to my people, I will not be here in spring.

"You are preparing to hunt the bear," she says. "It won't do you any good. You won't even make it to her cave. And your people are dead forever."

"No," I say. "You do not know this." Even the shaman cannot say what will happen. He can say what the spirits want to happen. But if a man can be stronger than the spirits, he can change the way of things.

Cynthia's cold eyes look deep inside me. "I know it will happen as I say."

"I am a good hunter," I say. "I am strong."

"But you have questions for me," she says, and when she smiles, her teeth are white and even. I know that her answers will weaken me. "You will never return to your people," she says. "It will happen as I see it."

"Why?" I ask, watching her eyes.

She shrugs. "That's the way the world works."

She is young, I realize now. Older than I am, but not as old as Amanda—*dark*. I remember that once I thought I knew how the world worked. Before I followed the bear into this world, I knew. I do not know anymore.

She does not understand the nature of the changing world—where ice can melt to water and water can become mist. I want to shake her belief in her own power.

"Roy Morgan came here and when he left he was different," I say.

"Roy changed, all right," she says. "I don't understand the nature of the change completely. But it doesn't really matter."

"You do not fear this difference?" I ask. Her face is

45

a little harder, a little colder and I think that she does fear. "Do you have questions too?" She does not speak, but her smile is gone. "Why did you come here?"

"I came to answer your questions, Sam," she says. "Besides, with so few cameras left, it's hard to watch from the outside."

So few cameras that watch? Does she mean the eyes?

"Yes, there are some left. You shouldn't figure you found them all so easily." She is sure of herself again, laughing at me.

I shake my head. She does not matter. "I will hunt the bear," I say.

"Yes," she says. "I know you will. But you won't win. You can't argue with the future, Sam." She turns away.

She steps into the snowmobile—not a beast, but a thing as dead and spiritless as a boulder. The scream rises from it and Cynthia runs away over the mountains.

The scent of oil lingers long after she is gone.

The fourth snowfall comes—not a gentle fall like the others, but a blizzard. The snow is driven by a cold wind that freezes the surface of the spring so that I must use a stone to break a hole in the ice. The tiny fire that I have built burns slowly and the hut smells of smoke.

I sit by the fire and I dream true dreams as I watch the flames. I wrap myself in the skin of the buck and I dream of winters past. I huddle with the rest of the herd and the snow forms a frost coat over my fur. My breath makes clouds that mingle with the breath of the herd.

I dream of my people. They are in the winter camp and the hut where my mother sleeps is warm. It smells of people and warmth and smoke. I call to my mother, but she does not hear me and the dream fades.

I dream of the bear, asleep in her cave. Her cave is warmed by her breath and filled with her scent. I stand beside her and lay my hand on her fur. She stirs in her sleep. "I will come to you, Great One," I say. "Soon, I will come." She grumbles in her sleep, but I do not understand what she says.

Seven days before the full moon, the storm passes. The Valley is white. The slopes of the mountains are covered with snow and the gray rock shows through in jagged lines. The mountains seem taller now.

I will hunt on the day of the full moon. Long ago, I prepared my spears and my knives for the hunt. Now I prepare myself. The shaman is not here to instruct me, but I know that I must show the proper respect to the spirit or the hunt will fail.

I use leafy branches and bark to build a small sweathouse by the side of the stream. The fire is hot within the house. When I throw water on the rocks by the fire, steam rises. I breathe the steam and it washes me clean. I crouch by the fire until I can stand the heat no longer, then I run into the snow and I wash in the stream, scooping water with my hands from the trickle that runs between snow banks. I cry out at the touch of the water, and the birds fly from the trees by the stream and the deer stare from far across the Valley.

Each morning, I chant to the spirits, asking for strength. I eat no meat; I eat only the berries and seeds that I stored before the snows came. I am strong— I will kill the bear and take her spirit. I will return to my world and tell my people of the strange world of the spirits. Perhaps I will become a shaman; perhaps a man of great power.

I awaken before dawn on the seventh day. Icicles— like knives—hang from the door of the sweathouse. I take my spear and my knives and I start across the Valley. My soft footsteps in the snow are the only sounds I hear.

I climb the slope, past the place where I buried a

watching eye. I think that I could walk forever like this. The world is silent and I am strong and sure. I follow the path that I followed last fall.

The sun looks over the rim of the mountains, and I reach a place where the snow blocks my way. White powder fills the gully where I climbed last fall. I climb around on the jagged gray rocks. The rocks are slick with ice, but I do not hesitate. This is my Valley and my hunt.

I climb higher. Once, I see the tracks of a cave lion crossing a patch of smooth snow. He is hunting, just as I am, in the gray dawn.

Higher on the mountain, I climb on bare rock. The snow that touched these rocks has melted in the light of day, then frozen again to make a sleek coating of ice. My moccasins slip once on the gray stone, and I catch myself with my hands. It would be easy to slide away down the slope, slipping on the smooth rock.

A raven flies above me, laughing. His laughter echoes in the stillness and I watch him fly. Laughing like Cynthia laughed. When he goes, it is silent again, except for the sound of my footsteps.

The way is steep here. The rock is shattered, broken by the snow of many winters and the sun of many summers. Steep, and some rocks are loose and ready to slide over the snow and away. I step carefully, testing each rock before I stand on it. A rock begins to slip beneath me and I step away. It shifts and slides, other rocks shifting with it. The snow and ice crack and cry in high-pitched voices, like the laughter of the raven. I stand still and the voices stop. The mountain is silent again.

I walk more carefully now, testing each step twice. The sun is up and the mountain is beginning to speak. I hear the small, shifting sounds of snow warming, melting a little, dripping, yielding. I have almost reached the path that leads to the bear's den.

I hurry now, thinking of how I will light the fire to

drive the bear out, of how I will return to my tribe and . . .

I hear a sound that does not fit in my Valley—a click, a whir. I look up and a metal eye watches me from the side of a boulder, watching me and my Valley. I step toward it, my spear held ready to strike. I am strong and I will destroy this eye as I have destroyed the others.

The rock shifts suddenly beneath my feet, freed of ice by the morning sun. I try to catch myself, but I have moved too suddenly, too quickly, and I slide with the rock. A pain traces its way up my leg—like the cut of a knife or an icicle or a shard of rock. I grab at rocks with my hands but they slip away. A rock rushes toward me and crashes against my head and then the world is dark.

The sun is warm on my face. I can feel rock—cold and unyielding—against my left side. My leg is twisted beneath me and the pain is a fiery line from my ankle to my thigh. I hear a raven laughing nearby and my head aches.

I open my eyes and see the blue sky above me. When I move, the raven flies away from the boulder beside me, sailing high over me into the sky that is his home.

I have no home.

My head aches; my leg aches. I am wedged between two boulders and I cling to one as I stand—putting all my weight on the leg that does not hurt. My right leg is crusted with old blood; when I straighten it, the blood flows fresh from the long cut. It was cut by a shard of rock or a jagged piece of ice; I do not know which and it does not matter.

I take a step and my leg gives beneath me. I catch myself on the boulder.

The place where I slipped is high above me. The sun is warm on my skin, but I am weak from the blood

49

that has trickled away. The bear sleeps in her cave, but I cannot hunt her, one-legged and weak as I am.

I pick my way up the slope—hobbling where I can, crawling where I must, leaving a spot of red each time my right leg touches the ground.

The eye is high on the side of the boulder, attached to the stone. I cannot pull it down. I cling to the side of the boulder—cold gray stone that is a part of the mountain that rises from my Valley. With a heavy rock in my right hand, I smash at the eye: once, twice—and with the strength of the mountain and the strength of my Valley—three times.

The clear glass that covers the eye breaks like the ice over the spring. The box clicks once, whirs once. I hit it again and it is silent. Dead, cold and spiritless.

I look down at the Valley far below. The mountain gives me strength. I wash my leg with snow, bind it with rabbit skins from one of my leggings, and begin to pick my way down the slope. The way back is a long one. But I know that I will reach my hut.

Roy Morgan is coming in spring. I will be there. Cynthia said so.

4

I hear a rifle's blast. The mountains echo the sound—over and over and over. Roy Morgan has come back to my Valley.

I stand on the bank of the stream. The first thaw of spring has melted much snow and the stream flows fast. The low plants that grow here have new shoots. In the meadow, beasts graze on small patches of new grass; the snow that covers the rest of the land is old and crusted. Spring is coming. The winter has been long and lonely.

Roy Morgan waits for me beside my hut. "You've been busy this winter," he says when he sees me. "The engineers had figured we might lose a few cameras to rockfalls—but not two-thirds of the ones we installed."

I stop a few paces from him, waiting and thinking of the hidden eyes that I have smashed or walled into hiding places.

"How's your leg?" he asks. He looks at the thin scar that stretches from my ankle to my knee. "It's healed well."

I watch him.

After a moment, he asks, "Aren't you going to say anything, Sam?"

"Has Amanda—*dark* come back?" I ask.

He laughs then, throwing back his head. I can hear the hyena spirit in the sound. "That's what I like about you, Sam. You're so damn stubborn. You just don't give up." He looks at me steadily. "I suppose you'll be going after the bear again now that your leg is healed."

I do not speak. I study his face. The hyena spirit is there—though it shows only in his eyes and in his laughter.

"I really don't know where Amanda is," he says. "If I did, I'd let her come and visit you here."

I do not know whether I should believe him. "Why are you here?" I ask.

"There is a man who wants to meet you. He and his son will be coming to the valley. . . ."

"Why?"

He frowns. "You don't know enough about the rest of the world to understand why he'd want to come here. I'm letting him come to the valley because he's contributed considerable sums of money to the Project and . . ."

51

"Money?" I ask. The word is unfamiliar. Amanda–*dark* never used it.

Roy Morgan shakes his head. "Never mind." He studies my face for a moment. "Ben's son is older than you are, but you might be friends." He shrugs. "Or you might not."

The winter has been long and lonely. Amanda–*dark* may have forgotten me by now. I would like to know other people—even the strange people of this world.

"Ben and his son will come here in three days," Roy Morgan says.

I nod. "I will meet them."

On the third day, I hide in a jumble of boulders near the Barrier. I can see Roy Morgan's boot prints in the old snow—a trail of prints where he entered the Valley, a trail where he left, passing between two of the tall, gray teeth. His tracks cross the Barrier as if nothing were there, but when I tried to walk the same path, I found the Barrier, solid as a wall of rock, blocking my way.

The morning passes. Birds fly over my head. A raven laughs at me from the top of a pine. I wait and I watch the Barrier.

The sun is overhead when I see two people coming. The older man has hair the color of flame. He is pale—paler than Roy Morgan, almost as pale as Cynthia. He walks with an awkward step—as if the snow were deep, though just a few inches remain on the ground.

A young man walks a few steps behind the red-haired man. His hair is the golden brown of meadow grass in the summer. He holds his head high as he walks—like a buck watching and listening for danger. He looks older than I am, but he seems wary, unsure of himself.

Without hesitating, they pass between the gray teeth that mark the Barrier. They pass me, following Roy

Morgan's winding trail down to the Valley. When they are out of sight, I test the Barrier between the gray teeth. It is solid as it has always been, and I wonder what power lets these people pass through this wall.

I follow a gully down to the Valley, a path much shorter than their winding trail. I go to the spring, where they are likely to come for water. Here, I wait.

I hear footsteps on the trail—one man, by the sound. I see him before he sees me—he is looking off into the bushes where a raven is laughing. Seeing him now, I remember a time that I moved in the uncertain way that he is moving, watched the world around me just as carefully as he is. I remember waking up in the room before I knew that it was called a room, and walking through the corridors with Amanda—*dark*. This man has stepped into a world that is not his own.

"Hello," I say.

He stops in the trail. His hand is on the handle of the knife at his belt. He studies me without speaking. His eyes are the color of the summer sky. He is taller than I am by at least two hands' widths. "I am Sam," I say. "I live here."

He relaxes a little, but his hand remains on the knife. "I suppose I could have figured that out. I'm Marshall."

I grin at him then, and hold out my hands to show that they are empty.

He takes his hand off his knife and grins back. "Sorry. This place makes me . . ." he begins. A bird— one of the blue birds that are so noisy—shrieks in the bushes beside him and he turns quickly to face the sound. "What's that?"

"Just a bird," I say. "There are no birds where you live?"

"Sounds like it's being strangled," he grumbles. "I've never heard a bird sound like that."

"Where do you live?" I ask.

He looks back at me, and when the bird shrieks again, he ignores it. "In the city," he says. "We've got sparrows and pigeons and street gangs and trouble, but no birds that sound like they're being killed in the bushes."

"What is the city?"

He shrugs. "Lots of people, lots of buildings, lots of cars. That's about it." He shakes his head. "You live out here alone? What do you eat?"

"I hunt. I find fruit and I trap rabbits. There are many foods here."

"Yeah? How do you trap rabbits?" He looks at the stone blade that dangles from my belt and the rabbit skins that I have sewn together for clothes. "I don't see. . . ."

"I will show you," I say.

Marshall follows me along the bank of the stream. Twigs snap beneath his boots; he brushes against bushes and grasses as he walks. Any beast could hear us. I turn and frown at him. "You walk like a moose," I say and I point out the sticks his boots have broken and the branches he has bumped. "You must walk more quietly," I say.

He frowns, but he walks more softly. I grin at him and say, "Now you are like a baby moose. Just a little smaller."

"Huh," he says. "I'd like to see you get across town without getting run over or beat up. Then we'd see who's a moose." But he is grinning.

The first trap is empty. The loop of braided sinew dangles in the rabbit trail, undisturbed. The second has been sprung by a passing deer. The third has caught a buck rabbit. I slit his throat. "This will be dinner," I say.

Marshall looks back toward the meadow. "I suppose my dad is setting up camp and wondering what happened to me." He shrugs. "He won't worry. He doesn't know how." Marshall pulls a pipe from a pouch at his belt. I know it is a pipe—the shaman of our tribe smoked a pipe in some ceremonies of power.

"Do you smoke?" Marshall asks.

"I do not know how," I say.

"I'll show you."

We sit by the stream and Marshall shows me how to suck smoke into my mouth and blow it out. The taste makes me cough, but I learn. This is not a ceremony, but it is a friendly custom. Marshall can blow rings of smoke and he says that if I teach him to walk quietly in the woods, he will teach me how to blow smoke rings.

Marshall leans back on his hands and watches me blow puffs of smoke. "How did you do that to your leg?" he asks, pointing to the scar.

I tell him about hunting the bear and finding the metal eye and falling in the rocks.

"You were hunting a bear alone?" He shakes his head. "You're nuts."

"I do not understand."

"Crazy. Bats." He is still shaking his head. "Why the hell would you hunt a bear by yourself?"

I frown. "I will hunt her again. I dreamed of the bear and I must hunt her." I explain about the spirits as well as I can. "The bear led me into the spirit world," I say.

"You mean here?" He looks around him. "I hate to break the news to you, Sam, but this isn't the spirit world. This is California. You're in the Sierras."

I shrug again and use words that Amanda–*dark* said often during Language Lessons. "Close enough."

He laughs. "Fine. But don't tell all the folks who live out there." He waves in the direction of the Barrier and takes the pipe. We sit in silence as he blows another set of smoke rings.

"What is it like where you live?" I ask. All I can see through the Barrier is more mountains.

"I live at a college in the city. I go to school. Now

55

and then, I fight in the street." He puffs on the pipe. "When he's around, my dad stops in to see me. But he's not around often. He's gone most of the time."

I do not understand the words he uses. I try to learn more. "Gone where?"

"To the moon. Or out to the asteroid belt. He owns Lunatic Mining Company—he started it back before anyone thought we'd ever use the moon for anything much." He leans back, the pipe in his mouth at a tilted angle. "He started with a tiny rig on the moon. Now he owns the ships that prospect the Belt and the main station that processes the ore and the small operations that work the moon. I want to head out into the Belt, learn to work on a small prospector or an ore-rig. I could do it. But my dad won't let me." He shrugs. "And I can't run away to space as long as he owns the ships."

The words are strange to me. "I do not understand."

"Neither do I," he says slowly. "Neither do I."

Only a smoldering ash remains in the pipe. Marshall taps it on the moss beside him and it turns black and dead. "I guess it's time to head back," he says.

He leads the way back to the spring. He walks carefully—still noisy, but better. Though I do not understand his words most of the time, I like him.

As we cross the meadow, I can see the bright orange of a shelter beside my hut. Marshall says that it is a tent.

The man with red hair meets us by the flat rock. He has built a small fire on the rock.

"I met Sam down by the spring," Marshall says. "We've got dinner—a rabbit." Marshall's voice is a little louder than it was by the stream; he speaks faster. "Sam, this is Ben, my father."

I nod.

"Glad to meet you, Sam," Ben says. He holds his hand out and I am not sure what to do. I put the rabbit in his empty hand. He looks half-puzzled, half-amused, but he takes the rabbit and runs a hand over the fur at its neck. "You snared it?" He looks at me and Marshall.

"Caught it in a loop of braided stuff," Marshall says.

"A snare," Ben says, nodding. "Set to spring when the rabbit hits it."

I am surprised. "You know how to trap rabbits?" I ask.

"No. But I've read about it. The Indians in the Yukon used to snare snowshoe hares that way."

I follow Ben and Marshall to the fire, and I wonder who the Indians are and where the Yukon is and whether I could go there and hunt with them.

I learn new words that night. Ben cooks the rabbit in a pot on a camp stove to make a stew. I eat as the others do, using a spoon to eat from a bowl of stew.

Twilight comes to the Valley. Ben pours a dark juice that he calls wine into my cup. Ben takes three rifles from the pack that he had carried into the Valley. He begins to clean one. Metal clicks against metal. In the dim light, the barrel of the rifle could almost be a part of the man's arm.

Far away from the camp, a saber-toothed cat shrieks. I see Marshall's shoulders stiffen. "The cat screams only after she has killed," I say to him softly. "If you hear her scream, you are all right." He relaxes again.

The full moon is rising over the Valley. "Does it look about the same as it did in your time, Sam?" Ben asks.

I study the round, white face of the moon. "The same," I say.

"There are men up there now," he says.

I shake my head. "Men of great power."

"No, ordinary men. Miners, mechanics, pilots . . . ordinary guys." He sets one rifle aside and picks up another. "And we've gone farther than the moon. Out to the asteroids. And we'll go farther still."

He says that the men on the moon are not men of

power, but I think that he is wrong. He does not understand the power that he has and that they must have.

For a moment, he looks up from the rifle that he is inspecting and studies my face. "You don't like Roy Morgan much, do you? I watched videotapes of the times he talked with you at the Project."

I nod. "I do not think he is a good man or a wise man."

"I wouldn't know about good or wise. But he kicked in money to help start our first mining operation on the moon. He dreams big and he dreams far. I don't know if he's a good man, but I respect him."

Ben waits for a moment for a reply, but I have nothing to say. He goes back to inspecting the rifle in his lap. "You and Marshall will both learn to shoot tomorrow," he says.

"Great," Marshall says and his voice is eager. I think that Marshall is braver than he is wise.

I shiver, remembering the blast of Roy Morgan's rifle. I do not think that I want to learn. "Are you cold?" Marshall asks.

I shrug. "Sometimes." Somehow, I do not want Marshall to know that I am afraid of the rifles. I do not think that he will understand if I explain that the weapon has no spirit and no right to take a life.

Marshall goes to his pack. "Here's a flannel shirt," he says. "I don't think my jeans would fit you."

The shirt is green. It is tight across my shoulders, but it fits. I put the rabbit skins over it. "Looks great," Marshall says.

I am warmer and the wind that had been blowing through the gaps between the rabbit skins no longer touches me. I thank Marshall for the shirt.

"Do you want to sleep in the tent tonight?" Marshall asks. "There's space if . . ."

"I will sleep where I always sleep," I say.

I lie beneath the overhanging rock where I awoke

on my first day in the Valley. I am warm—wrapped in Marshall's shirt and in the skin of the buck who gave me his spirit. I think of too many things—of rifles and power and men on the moon. The moon watches me. And at last, I sleep.

It is dawn and the day is cold. The snow has frozen into a hard crust once again. Spring is not yet here.

Though I walk lightly in the footprints of days past, the snow crackles beneath me. I hear rustling inside the tent and Marshall looks out. He motions me to wait and, a moment later, he crawls out of the tent and goes with me to the spring.

We must break a thin layer of ice to get to the water and Marshall shivers as I take a long morning drink from cupped hands. "We'll have to get the stove started so we can make coffee," he says.

"Coffee?" I ask.

"You'll find out," he says. "You probably won't like it much. Most people don't, at first."

He pushes his hands into the pockets of his jeans and stands by the spring. He does not head for the stove and this thing called coffee. "You know, I don't much like Roy Morgan, either," Marshall says. "I don't care what my dad thinks."

I nod.

Marshall still does not move, still stands with his hands in his pockets. "You don't want to learn to shoot a rifle, do you?" he asks.

"I have seen Roy Morgan's rifle and I do not like it," I say.

"But if you are going to hunt animals like bears, you really should know how to shoot," he says. "Or take along someone who knows how to shoot." Then he grins suddenly. "You see?"

"You want to go hunting with me?"

"If you're going hunting and if you decide you want company," he says.

I nod slowly.

"Think about it," he says quickly, then takes his hands out of his pockets and walks back up to the flat rock and the camp stove. Ben is already heating water in a pot for coffee.

Coffee is a bitter drink that tastes like one of the shaman's cures—but I drink a cup because it is warm. We eat eggs that Ben has cooked. I do not understand why he cooks eggs, since they are so easy to eat raw, but I do not ask.

And we go to the meadow to learn to shoot. Ben sets five rocks on top of a boulder, then we walk many steps away from the rocks. Ben gives each of us a rifle to hold.

I do not like to hold the rifle. I remember the bitter smoke that lingered in my Valley after Roy Morgan killed the hyena. I remember the bark of the rifle and the echo from the mountains. I remember how birds fly away from the rifle's blast, how the deer and grazing beasts run away.

"Stop frowning, Sam," Ben says. He has been explaining how to use the rifle. I have not been listening. "It's a tool—nothing more than that. You can use it for good or for bad, just like any other tool."

I nod slowly. Ben is a man of great power, even if he does not know that power. I will listen to him—at least for now.

Marshall tries first. I watch as Ben adjusts the position of his son's hands on the rifle, shows Marshall where to look, warns him what to expect. The rifle's blast is just as I remembered; the smoke burns my nostrils. Marshall frowns, rubbing his shoulder, and Ben says, "Again." Marshall shoots again. And again. And again. The five rocks—all in a row—are still on the boulder when he is done.

Then Ben's hands are warm on mine, showing me how to hold the rifle. "Now," he says, and I squeeze the trigger as he tells me to. The rifle kicks my shoulder. The blast and the smoke are worse because they are so near me.

"Again," he says.

Through the sights I can see one of the five stones. I squeeze the trigger. The rifle kicks; my ears ring with the sound and still the stone is atop the boulder.

"Again."

The same.

"Once more."

This time I can see the puff of dust when the bullet hits the boulder. The blast does not hurt my ears as much; my shoulder is already sore.

Marshall shoots. Then I shoot. Then Marshall shoots. Sometimes, we hit the rocks. When all five are down, Ben sets them back again. I hit the rocks more often than Marshall. He is still stiff and tense. When he pulls the trigger, he jerks the gun. The more he misses, the stiffer his shoulders are.

Marshall misses again, and lowers his rifle. Ben studies his son's face for a moment. "You've got to relax with it," Ben says. He raises his rifle and gently pulls the trigger. A rock spins away. Ben lowers the rifle and pats Marshall's shoulder. "Just think of it as a chance to learn more about your own strengths and weaknesses."

Marshall is watching a raven in a distant tree. "Yeah," he says.

Ben frowns a little. "Why don't you two keep practicing? I'll make lunch."

Marshall continues watching the raven as his father walks away. He glares at the boulder and the rocks and lifts his gun. A rock spins away when he fires. He lowers his rifle, still frowning.

"Hell of a lot he knows about strengths and weaknesses," Marshall says in a growl. "He has no weaknesses." He looks toward the camp. "I can't do anything right when he's around."

I watch Marshall. I do not understand what has happened between Marshall and Ben.

"And I can't get far enough away from him to do something right on my own," Marshall says.

Marshall's shirt is warm around my shoulders. The air is cold. I know by the scent in the wind that the day will get colder before it gets warmer. "This is the right kind of day to hunt the bear," I say softly. "Cold enough to keep her in her den until the hunters drive her out with smoke." My leg aches in the cool air.

Marshall sets the rifle butt on the ground and studies my face.

"We must walk half a day to get to her den," I say. "We could leave before dawn tomorrow, before Ben is awake." I stop for a moment, watching his face. He is starting to grin. "Come with me," I say. "But remember—the kill will be mine. The bear is mine."

He is grinning now. "All yours," he says. "I'm just along for the ride." He takes the pipe from its pouch and packs the leaves that he calls tobacco into its bowl. "So tell me about how you hunt the bear."

We smoke; we shoot; after a time, we eat lunch. Marshall grins and the air is sharp with more than the cold. I feel a tension, a waiting feeling that hangs in the air like smoke from the pipe.

I can feel the tension when we sit at the fire that evening. And I know that Ben can feel it. Marshall watches the fire dance and he grins at nothing.

"When I was your age, or maybe a little younger, my dad took me deer hunting as a kind of rite of passage," Ben says.

"Yeah?" says Marshall, still staring into the fire. "What's a rite of passage?"

Ben frowns impatiently. "When a boy becomes a man, that's a rite of passage." He watches Marshall watch the fire. "There aren't many places left to hunt deer."

"I can think of a rite of passage," Marshall says. He

looks up from the fire to meet his father's eyes. "Send me on a prospector in the Belt. That'd be a rite of passage."

"You're not ready for that yet," Ben says.

"How do you know that?" Marshall says. "You're home for a week or a day or maybe two weeks, then you're off again. How would you know?" His voice is matter-of-fact; not accusing, just telling Ben about his life.

"I have to be out there," Ben says softly. "That's my business, that's my world. . . ."

"All right," Marshall says softly, staring into the fire. "That's your world. But don't think you know about me."

We go to sleep early that night. Marshall and I leave the fire before the flames have died. Ben sits up much later—far into the night, I can see the light of the flames through the trees.

The sky is still dark when I reach into the orange tent and touch Marshall's shoulder. He jerks awake and I lay my hand over his mouth before he can speak. He slips quietly from the tent. Together, we cross the meadow to the bare rock of the mountain, where no one will be able to follow our trail. Marshall takes dry meat from the pack that he carries and we chew it as we walk.

"Ben will not be able to track us on the rock," I say softly.

"He probably won't follow," Marshall says. "I left a note that said we'd be back tonight. So maybe he'll just wait for us."

I can feel the chill of the mountain through my moccasins. The rocks high on the mountain's slope are touched with the gray light of dawn.

We rest on the side of the mountain and we smoke Marshall's pipe. I wonder—Marshall is my friend, but he is not a member of my tribe. To hunt together, we should be of the same tribe. "We should be brothers," I say to him.

He frowns. "What do you mean?"

"Blood brothers. If we are to hunt together. . . ."

"How do you do it?"

The tribe should be with us to accept a new member. The shaman should chant, a feast should be made. But there is no tribe and no shaman—there is only me.

We use his sharp metal knife to cut my arm, my stone blade to cut his. Drops of our blood fall to the rock and form a pool. I chant to the spirits, telling them of my friendship with Marshall, asking them to take him as a member of my tribe, blood brother to me. And it feels right.

I say to Marshall, "It is done."

He hands me the sharp steel knife. "You should keep this," he says. "I'd like you to."

The blade of the knife catches the rays of the sun and reflects them back with a red glow. This is a good knife—sharp and thirsty for blood. I give him my stone blade.

A little uncertain of ourselves in the new day and the new brotherhood, we climb the slope. We pass two hidden eyes that I have walled in and I point them out to Marshall. I lead Marshall around the place that I fell, following a longer, but safer, path.

"Remember," I say to Marshall as we come to the narrow path that leads to the bear's den. "The kill is to be mine."

He nods. His eyes are bright now, excited. "I just stay out of the way."

He should not be excited. To hunt, a man must relax and become a part of the mountain. "You will watch," I say. I explain how we will pile brush by the mouth of the den. When we light it, the smoke will drive the bear out—sleepy and confused. I will meet her with spear and knife.

64

"There is a ledge where you can stand, out of the way."

"And if it looks like the bear is going to get you, then . . ."

"No," I say. "You will watch. The bear is mine."

He frowns, but he nods. He should not be excited; he does not know how to be a part of the mountain. But I am glad to have him here. My leg aches in the chill of the morning, but I can ignore it when I talk to Marshall.

The path is drifted with snow. We carry dry brush and pile it by the cave's low mouth. The air from the den breathes of bear—a warm, musty smell. We leave only a narrow opening for the bear to pass through, blocking the rest with brush.

I am ready to hunt. I am as calm as the stone beneath my feet. Marshall stands up above the cave mouth, on the narrow ledge below the hidden eye.

I light the brush, using what Marshall calls a match. The brush flares and the smoke drifts into the cave. I stand ready—my spear in one hand, the sharp steel knife in the other. I hear a rumbling sound within the cave—like heavy breathing. I hear claws on stone, and movement. The smoke drifts, and again I hear the rumbling sound.

"Is anything happening?" Marshall calls down to me. "What? . . ."

I hear a growl; I hear the scratch of claws on stone; I smell the musty scent of bear. She comes—so fast—charging through the low mouth. The burning brush scatters before her and smoke surrounds us both. She backs away from the burning branches, growling and shaking her head as if to clear the smoke from her eyes. She sees me and lunges, swatting at me with angry paws. I aim a spear thrust at her throat, but a paw knocks it aside. I strike her shoulder, but the point only scratches her. I step back and she howls into the smoky air.

Smoke, fire, cold stone, cold air—I am alive now, alert, hunting as I should be hunting. The pain in my leg is gone.

So fast—she lunges again, charging through a clump of burning brush. I dodge back from her claws and bright teeth. I thrust again with the spear and catch her in the shoulder. The spearpoint sticks firmly and she rips the spear from my hands when she rears back to howl and tear at the spear with her other paw. The spear dangles from her shoulder and blood darkens her fur.

She is angry, maddened. She shakes her head, snapping her jaws at the smoke in the air as she would at a swarm of flies. Her eyes are red, half-closed and bleary from smoke. She drops back and the spear is still in her shoulder.

She will charge again, I know. She cannot see clearly in the smoke. If I dodge to the side when she comes for me, if she charges fast in the smoky air . . . the ledge ends abruptly and the rocks below are sharp. She starts to charge, but she follows me when I dodge. I kick burning brush into her path and she howls when she steps on hot embers. Above me, as though it were far away, I hear the blast of a rifle.

I cannot stop to shout at Marshall. The bear is lunging for me—fast, so fast—and I step to the side and she starts to turn for me, starts to slip on the edge.

The rifle blasts. I smell the smoke. And the bear falls, over the edge to the rocks below. A bright flower of blood is beside her eye; the fur of her head is sprayed with red. "No," I say as she falls. "No. She was to be mine."

I stand on the edge, still holding the knife. She lies on the rocks below. Still, my spear dangles from her shoulder. "Are you all right?" Marshall shouts from above. "Are you? . . ."

I do not answer. I scramble down the loose rock

beside the path to stand beside the bear. One eye is open, staring blankly at the sky. The other is covered by a film of blood. I can see the wound where the bullet entered.

"Sam!" Marshall scrambles down the rocks to stand beside me. "You all right?" I do not speak. "She's enormous," he says. "I didn't think. . . ." He lets the words trail off.

"The kill was to be mine," I say softly.

"But she was going to kill you," he says. "I couldn't just watch." He believes what he is saying. "You just had a knife. I couldn't just watch. . . ." He is shaking his head. "You're mad that I killed her?"

I do not know what to do. "You killed her. Her spirit is yours."

"What?" he says. "But you . . ."

"I did not kill the beast," I say angrily. "Her spirit is yours. You must take her spirit as your own. I have no right to it."

"I don't understand." He puts a hand on my shoulder and I step back so that it falls away.

Stupid people. Stupid. The air around us is sharp and cold. I followed this bear; we were linked. But I cannot take her spirit—I have no right. I throw back my head and howl—like a wolf at the moon, like a cat at a kill. I have no words for this, no words, only the howling wailing cry. I hold the bright steel knife in my hand and the world around me is sharp and bitter. Marshall steps back, away from me. I wail—the voice is great within me, but there are no words.

I kneel and I slash the throat of the bear with the bright blade. The spirit rises, large and angry. But I am angry too. "He is here, the one who killed you," I shout in the Old Tongue. "But he is a child—he does not know you, he does not want you."

The spirit roars. She is angry. She was not prepared to die. She was not treated with respect. She swings a hazy paw at my head and I duck away. She shakes her head, confused, and sniffs at the body at her feet.

"I am not the hunter here, Great One. But I will take you." I reach for her as the shaman would reach for a beast spirit, but she rears back and roars. She growls, the grumbling of a beast that has awakened too soon from a winter sleep.

"Come to me, Great One," I tell her in the Old Tongue. "This one is not ready for you." She shakes her heavy head. I am no shaman—I cannot make her come to me.

Marshall stands a few steps away. His face is bewildered and his eyes are wide—but they watch me, not the spirit.

The smoke of the fire drifts around us, around the spirit, and she lifts her head to smell the smoke. The smoke becomes darker; she steps away with the cloud of drifting smoke. I lose sight of her in the smoke. She is gone—for now. This is bad. This is wrong. This is not as it should be.

I kneel and I cut the big claws from her powerful front paws. With the sharp knife, I cut two strips of skin from the soft skin at her throat, and I scrape the fur from them. I make holes in the claws and I string them on the strips of skin.

Marshall is watching. "Sam," he says at last, "I don't understand what you're doing."

I go to him with the strip of skin and the dangling claws. "You do not understand and I cannot explain it all," I say wearily. I put the claws around his neck and say, "Wear these. They may protect you if the spirit comes back." The shaman used claws and teeth to give a hunter power over animals. I do not know that this will work against the bear spirit, but I must try.

I wear the other set of claws myself.

We leave the bear. We leave the smell of blood and gunpowder. We leave the cold mountainside to walk the long way back to the Valley. I am numb. I do not want to talk. My leg aches and I am cold.

We can see the orange tent below. Marshall stops at the foot of the mountain and puts his hand on my shoulder. The claws dangle around his neck and the bloody thong has left a red streak on his skin. "I'm sorry, Sam."

His eyes are still blue as the sky; his shirt is still warm on my back. "We are brothers, Marshall," I say. "But I wish you had understood."

We go to the tent together—weary, dirty, marked with blood.

Ben greets us with a roar of anger. There are many words exchanged, shouts, explanations—and I do not understand most of it. Ben shouts about ". . . irresponsible! Stupid, crazy . . ." and Marshall explains many things very quickly. Ben fingers the claws that dangle around Marshall's neck, and his face is changed. He says the same words, but his voice is softer and his hand rests on Marshall's shoulder.

I have nothing to say. Ben pats my shoulder too and says, "Thanks for bringing him back in one piece, Sam." I do not understand, but I do not want to understand.

Tomorrow, Ben says, they will return to the Outside. That night, I sleep beneath the overhang and watch the light of the fire dance. I can hear Ben's voice and Marshall's voice and I wonder what he tells his father. But I do not want to go to the fire and listen.

I sleep and I dream of the spirit of the bear. It is not a vision, not a true dream. The bear is gray and enormous—she floats and changes like smoke, changing like Marshall's smoke rings change when the breeze blows.

I awaken early, knowing that the bear spirit wanders in my Valley, looking for a home.

I walk with them to the Barrier. Marshall says, "I'll be back, Sam. As soon as I can. I'll be back."

I nod but I do not trust his words. Amanda—*dark* said that she would be back. Ben walks through the Barrier; Marshall follows, and turns to wave. They walk away toward the Outside.

And I am alone in the Valley with the spirit of the bear.

2

Dancing with Shadows

5

The Valley looks no different than it looked before Marshall and I hunted the bear. The snow is melting slowly; new green shoots grow by the stream.

But there is a tension in the air. There is a tension in me. I sit by the fire each night and I wait—like a child waiting for the hunters to return to camp. But the Valley is quiet. I wait by my fire alone and the mountains stare down at me. The signs of spring bring me no joy.

At last I know that I cannot stay here, by my warm fire in my rich Valley. The time has come to leave. There is only one place for me now.

I go to the cave of the bear.

Vultures have ripped at the bear's carcass, tearing the flesh away from the back and legs. Foxes, wildcats and other beasts have worried at the bones. The sun has dried the tatters of flesh and fur. The beasts will return and scatter the bones. The ravens will pick away the dry scraps of meat. The winter snow will cover the bare bones and, when it melts, carry them away in rushing streams of water. The carcass will be gone, but still the spirit will wander the Valley.

Ravens have pecked the eyes away and the bear watches me with empty sockets. The smell of death lingers here.

I sit on the ledge by the cave with my legs crossed beneath me and my hands on my thighs. Somewhere in the Valley, the bear spirit wanders. She may find me here. But I do not think so. I am waiting for death.

I do not know what happens to a person who dies in the world of the spirits. I will know soon, I think.

The sun rises higher in the sky. I do not move. The sunshine is warm on my back, but my legs ache where they rest against the cold rock. The scar throbs with a biting pain that comes and goes and comes and goes— as rhythmic as my heartbeat.

By the time the moon rises, the pain in my legs is gone. My legs are as cold as the rock. I am hungry and my back and shoulders are cold and sore. But I wait, not moving, and the hunger goes away. I am part of the mountain.

I hear the click of claws against rock. A fox passes near me on the ledge. He stops by the narrow path to look back at me. His fur is silver in the moonlight; his eyes glow.

I try to speak to him—to say good-bye to him and to this Valley. But my throat is dry and no words come. He turns away, slinking down through the rocks to where the carcass of the bear lies.

I am a part of the mountain. I close my eyes to sleep, and I do not think that I will awaken.

I am walking in a meadow and there is green grass beneath my feet. The wind carries the sharp, clean scent of the ice fields. A stream babbles nearby, flowing from ice fields that melt a little each spring but never melt entirely. The sun is low in the sky.

I know where I am.

I walk toward my tribe's springtime camp. I can see the tracks of small children by the stream. I remember when I ran and played here, chasing darting fishes in the shallow waters, throwing pebbles at boulders to test my aim, running over the rough ground until my heart was near bursting. I remember this.

I follow the path through the low trees. I hear voices

before I see the camp. Children are playing a chanting game; they shout the same words over and over in a rhythm that I remember. I smell a cook fire and roasting meat.

My mother sits by the fire with my aunt and my sister. My nephew and two young cousins play in a spot where sunlight shines down through the trees. My uncle and his wife sit together by the doorway to the hut, talking quietly. The other men sit together. My father is binding a spearpoint to a shaft; my cousin is talking; the shaman and the others are listening to him. He might be talking about the day's hunt, about a dream, about anything.

"I am here," I say. "I have come back." The words of my people feel unfamiliar when I speak. "I have come back from the world of the spirits."

My mother is the first to come to me. She lays a hand on my shoulder and she cries out in joy: "He is not a spirit," she calls out to the others. "He is here." And she hugs me and all the tribe comes to me, and each person must touch me and stroke my arms and ask me questions in the words that seem familiar and strange at the same time.

I stroke my mother's hand. Dark eyes she has—darker than even Amanda—*dark*'s eyes, I see now. Her hand is dry and her face has more wrinkles than I remembered. My youngest cousin has crept close and I stroke his head. He is older than I remember.

So many questions—I say that I have been to the world of the spirits and I can see that the shaman is watching me. He studies the claws that dangle around my neck, the scar on my leg, the bright metal knife that dangles from my belt.

". . . a feast," my mother is saying. "You are back with new strength and a new name and . . ."

"First there must be questions," the shaman says softly, and his voice cuts through the babble of the tribe. "There are many questions to be answered."

My mother's hand is warm on my shoulder, but I am cold. The shaman watches me steadily; his eyes calm and cool as a lake in the ice fields.

We sit in a circle around the fire. The meat that had been roasting has been forgotten. My mother takes it away to save for the feast. If there is to be a feast. One of my cousins puts wood on the fire, so that it flares brighter. The sunlight is almost gone.

I tell them of the spirit world. I tell them of the room and of Amanda—*dark* and of my new name. The sky is dark and the wind is cold. I tell of Roy Morgan and of the Valley and of my hunt for the buck. I tell them of the hyena spirit and the older men shake their heads at Roy Morgan's foolishness, but no one speaks. I show them my scar and I tell of the eyes on the mountain and my first hunt for the bear. I tell of Marshall and our hunt for the bear. The fire burns before me, but I am cold as I tell these things. The shaman watches me. And I tell of sitting by the cave of the bear, waiting. I tell it all, leaving nothing important from the tale.

When I am done, there are questions. Questions about the Valley, about the rifles and the metal knives, about the matches and the camp stove. But the shaman does not ask questions—he watches me. I tell people as much as I know—but there are many questions that I cannot answer. I do not know how the rifles worked, I only know they did. I do not know how the matches brought fire so quickly, though I can describe the smell and the sound and the feel of them.

The others are silent at last, and the shaman speaks. "You left the spirit of the bear alone in the Valley," he says. I nod. "That is not good." He is studying my face. "You did not make peace with her. She is still angry."

"I did not know how to make peace," I say. "I am not a shaman."

He shrugs. "You learn how by trying," he says. "Then you know how."

I look to my mother. The firelight shines in her dark eyes and she does not speak. The sharp points of the claws are pricking my chest. "I am not a shaman," I say again. "I did not want to try."

The shaman does not speak. He watches me and I am cold and alone in the circle of my tribe. "Must I go back?" I ask. "I want to stay here with my people."

He does not speak. The fire flares and crackles but the sound seems far away.

"I did not ask to go to the spirit world," I say. "I do not want to be a shaman. I . . ."

"It is not a question of asking or wanting," he says.

"Could I bring harm to the tribe by staying here?" I ask. "Could the bear spirit do harm?"

"She is an angry spirit," he says. "And you are not done with her yet. No shaman knows what an angry spirit can do."

I look around the circle at the faces of my tribe—dark skin, strong brows, dark eyes—my people. The firelight dances in my mother's eyes.

"I must go back," I say.

It is dark, getting darker, though the fire still burns and flares. The shaman's eyes are getting brighter and I cannot see the rest of the tribe around us. The world is getting darker and my mother and father and all the tribe are lost in the shadows.

"I do not want to go," I say. The smell of the fire is gone. The air is cold. I sit alone with the shaman in a dark place.

"I know," he says.

I look into his deep, still eyes and I wonder what he was like when he was young. Did he want to be a shaman? Did he want to lead the tribe?

"I will make peace with the bear," I say. "Then, maybe, I can come back."

He shakes his head slowly. "I do not think you will find your way back. And if you do, we may not be here. The beasts are moving and the ice is retreating and we will move with them. Who can say where we will travel?"

"In the spirit world, they said that all my people were dead and gone," I say. "But you are not dead. You are here." I reach out and I touch his wrinkled hand. Yes, he is here, but the world is dark and I can no longer see his face.

"I am old," he says. "I have learned many things, but I do not know all the ways of this spirit world. Perhaps, for them, we are dead."

"No," I protest.

"Perhaps," he says again, and his voice is further away. "You will learn for yourself, Sam. You will learn." Then, more distant still. "Go in peace, brother."

And he is gone. I am alone in the darkness.

Warm air smelling of strange smells. The clatter of metal on metal. Not rock beneath me, but softness. Soft blankets over me.

I hear a voice raised in protest—Roy Morgan's voice. I cannot understand the words, not yet. I feel like I have been swimming beneath the water in a cold lake, and I am only now rising to the air.

Another voice speaks, replying to Roy Morgan. This voice is as gray as the stone of the mountain. Solid. Lacking the bright edge and urgency of Roy Morgan's voice.

Roy Morgan speaks again, and this time I hear some of the words. "... you can see that he's well cared for. I don't see ..."

"Mr. Morgan, I have explained to you a number of times now that when the Court receives a complaint, we investigate. Moses recommended ..."

Roy Morgan's voice is sharp. "I have nothing but respect for that thinking machine of yours, but I wonder if all available data were submitted. That letter was from a nineteen-year-old boy, who ..."

The dull voice continues, as if Roy Morgan had not spoken. ". . . recommended an investigation. Since we have found justification for continuing our investigation, we will do so. And if we find that a hearing is needed to bring justice to . . ."

"Yeah," Roy Morgan says. "I understand."

"You wouldn't have to hear the answer so often if you didn't ask the question again and again," the voice says in a complaining tone. For a moment, there is silence. Then the voice speaks quickly, confidently. "Of course, we'll move him as soon as it's safe to do so. And then . . ."

"I still don't understand why the Court . . ." Roy Morgan begins again in a tired voice.

"Because you've taken an intelligent member of another species and you've treated him like chattel."

"You don't understand," Roy Morgan says. "I am building a world. A new world where there is more space and more adventure and more . . . just more." His voice is soft. "Sometimes I make mistakes."

"So Sam was a mistake and you treated him badly and . . ."

"Sam is my friend," Roy Morgan says.

I open my eyes. White wall meets white ceiling in a straight line. Four walls, four corners. I cannot escape this world.

The man who stands by Roy Morgan at the foot of my bed is frowning. He looks as if he always frowns. His hair is gray; his face is lined with wrinkles.

"I must go back to the Valley," I say, and both men look at me in surprise.

"You're awake," says Roy Morgan. "We had to bring you here, Sam. You were dying up there—exposure, starvation . . ."

I do not speak. I wait for him to finish.

The gray man steps forward. "Hello, Sam. I've been sent by the World Court to investigate your case. My name is Andrews, James Andrews." He looks at me as though he expects me to reply, but I do not speak. I have nothing to say to this man. "We received a letter from Marshall Dustan," Andrews says. "Mr. Dustan claimed that Mr. Morgan has not granted your rights under . . ."

I speak past the gray man to Roy Morgan. "Where is Marshall?"

"He is out in the Belt," Roy Morgan says. "He went out with Ben right after they returned from the Valley."

Andrews has stopped talking. His frown has become more unpleasant. "Mr. Dustan has been summoned for a hearing," he says now. He speaks slowly and loudly, as though he were talking to a stupid child. "He should be back for the hearing."

"You can't summon a man from the Belt," Roy Morgan says. "If he wants to be here, he'll be here. Your jurisdiction doesn't . . ."

"Don't tell me about . . ." Andrews begins.

"I must go back to the Valley," I say to the white walls and the white ceiling, but no one listens. I close my eyes and the voices fade to distant squabbling, like ravens fighting over a scrap of food. For a while, this world goes away.

6

I dream of the bear. She is wandering the Valley, searching for me—but I am not there. The mountains echo with her growls. This is not a true dream—I know even as I dream that I am lying in a warm room and not walking in the Valley. But I also know that in my Valley, the bear spirit is waiting.

The growls of the bear turn to the growls of a gruff voice, of two grumbling voices. ". . . late for the changing of the guard," one voice is grumbling.

"You make it sound like a military maneuver. I don't see why this one caveman matters so much that we have to sit with him morning, noon and . . ."

"You don't see," says the first voice heavily. "That's why you're an aide of an aide of an aide to the Court, and likely to remain so."

I open my eyes. Wall meets ceiling in a straight line. The man who is talking has short brown hair and a square chin. The man he is talking to has short black hair and a square chin.

"I must go back to my Valley," I say.

They look at me, startled. "Nurse," one calls out. The one who is sitting in the chair stands up.

I start to sit up, but my body is weak and the room spins—straight lines shifting, moving, twisting.

"I must go to the Valley," I say. There is a tube in my arm, heavy blankets over me. Still, the room spins.

"I don't think you're going anywhere for a while," one man says. "I think . . ."

The woman who bursts into the room is dressed in white. She moves with the speed and abruptness of the little birds that live in the grass. But her face is fierce. The men step back as she steps toward me.

She puts her hands on my shoulders and easily pushes me back down. She checks the tube on my arm, rearranges the pillow under my head, and says, "You speak English, right?"

I nod.

"Then listen. You're going to regret it if you start moving. You're not ready to go anywhere. So lie quiet and stay in bed." She whirls to face the two men. "And what the hell were both of you doing in here at

80

the same time? Bad enough having one at a time, getting in the way."

She does not give them time to answer; she turns back to me. Behind her, I see one man shaking his head as the other slinks from the room.

"And why were you trying to get up, anyway?" she growls.

She stops then, waiting for an answer. I study her—her lips are painted with red; around her eyes, she is painted with a blue that shines like the scales of a fish in the sun. Her hair is short and dark and she is small. But I know from the memory of her hands on my shoulders that she is strong.

"I must go back to the Valley," I say.

She studies me and shakes her head. "You won't be going anywhere for a while. First, you have to recover. Then, you have to deal with Moses and the Court." She jerked her head at the man who sat quietly behind her. "He'll tell you about that." Still, she makes no move to leave. "Tell me—why were you sitting out on a rock ledge in the middle of winter, anyway?"

The man behind her sits up straighter. "How did you know where? . . ." he begins.

"Hey, the hospital rumor network has Moses beat for info transfer," she says, without turning around. And she waits for my answer.

"I wanted to leave that place," I say.

She nods. "I can understand that one. You still want to die?"

I shake my head.

"Good," she says. "If you change your mind, don't do it on my shift." She starts to turn away.

"Wait," I say. I trust this woman more than I trust the two strange men. "Will you be back?"

She tilts her head when she looks at me. "I'll bring you dinner tonight. If you feel like eating."

"I will eat," I say.

She nods and she hurries away, leaving me with the

square-chinned man. He is uncomfortable talking to me, this man. He does not sit still—he shifts in his chair, his hands pick at his clothes, he does not look at my face. His name is . . . his name is not important.

Though he answers my questions, I do not understand his answers. I ask when I will return to the Valley, and he says that first I must sit before Moses and the Court. I ask who Moses is and though he answers, I do not understand. He says that Moses is a computer. "Or an information-processing system, really. Moses was programed to analyze world trends and systems. Economics, social trends, population changes, weather patterns, technological developments and their repercussions. Data from all over the world are entered in . . ."

He continues to talk, but I stop listening. I do not understand the words, but I think that even if I knew the words I might not understand. This man talks as if someone told him the words to say and he is only repeating them.

Other men and women come to see me this day. A man called the doctor asks me how I feel and takes blood from my arm with a needle. James Andrews comes to my room and tells me his name again. "I know who you are," I say. I do not like this place that the aide calls a hospital and I do not like Andrews. He speaks slowly and carefully as though I were a child. He repeats the same things that he told me when I first met him, and they make as little sense this time. I notice that after he leaves, the young man who has been sitting in my room begins to speak more carefully when he speaks to me. After a time, another young man comes and the first young man leaves. I do not ask their names. I do not like them and they are not important.

The birdlike woman in white comes back, with a tray of food for me. She smiles at the young man, and her face changes. She looks less fierce. "If you'd like to take a couple of minutes to go get dinner, I can cover for you," she says. "This is my last stop for the evening."

They talk for a minute, then the young man leaves. The woman sits in his chair and stretches her legs out in front of her. "What a day!" She links her hands behind her head and watches me for a moment. "You know how to use a fork and a knife?" she asks.

I nod. She has put the tray before me and I am studying the food. I eat with the fork as Marshall and Ben did.

"You'll do okay," she says after a moment. "But you don't have to use the fork on the bread. Use your hands for that."

"Thanks," I say, then stop. "My name is Sam. I do not know your name."

"Call me Zee," she says. She pulls a packet from the pocket of her white pants and unwraps it. "Chocolate," she says. "Want a piece?" She breaks off a piece of the dark brown stuff.

Zee is watching me again, her blue eyes steady on me. The chocolate has a strange, sweet taste.

"Like it?" she asks. "It's the real stuff. I have expensive tastes. If I could give up my expensive habits I could spend more time out of this place. But if I'm not spending money on chocolate, it's something else."

I watch her. I do not think she really wants an answer to her question. So I ask her the question that I have asked everyone I have seen this day. "Do you know when I will go back to my Valley?"

She shakes her head at me, frowning. "I'm only the nurse, Sam. They don't tell me Moses' secrets."

Though I asked the aide, I still do not know who Moses is. I ask Zee.

Still she frowns. "Who's Moses? Depends on who you ask. Guys like that lawyer, Andrews, act like he's God. Lot of people say he's just a big dumb machine, only as smart as the scientists who programed him." She shrugs. "I sure don't know. Maybe you'll find out in Court." For a moment, she is silent, watching me. Then she says abruptly, "You were half frozen when they brought you in here. I hear you were sitting out on a ledge in the snow." She studies my face. "Why did you do that?"

I shrug. "I needed to leave that place and there was nowhere else to go. Nothing else to do."

She is nodding then. "Yeah, I can understand that. That fish of a lawyer, Andrews, he wouldn't understand. But I understand. I'd like to leave this city, but there's nowhere else to go."

She is silent for a moment and I study her face. The other women who visited me this day had painted their lips and eyes, but not as brightly as Zee. She is different from the others.

"I've heard about your Valley," she says. "I've heard a little. Are there wolves there? I've never seen wolves, except in the zoo."

"There are wolves," I say.

"Tell me about them." She leans forward now, her eyes intent on me.

"Why?" I ask. "What do you want to know?"

She hesitates then, the first time I have seen her hesitate. She glances toward the door and back to me. "I hunt," she says softly, "in the streets at night. They don't know, here in the hospital, but I'm a knife-fighter." She lifts the cuff of her pants leg and shows me a knife, sheathed and bound to her shin. When she draws the knife, the blade flashes wickedly in the light. "The dulls don't like knife-fighters. They know we're crazy." She grins, just for a moment, then hides the knife again. "There are stories about us, about the knife-fighters. Stories in the newspapers and on the TV. They say we're like wolves. But I've never seen a wolf. The animals in the zoo are just like big dogs and that's not it. I want to know what wolves are like."

"What do you hunt for?" I ask her.

"A way out," she says and she is not smiling now.

84

"The only one we have found is the same one that you found." Her eyes are bright and hard. "They don't understand." She makes a gesture and I know she means the court aides, the doctors, all the rest of the world that I do not know. "They don't understand and they ask God and Moses where the hell we came from." She shrugs. "I don't believe there's a God, and Moses doesn't have any answers."

I do not think I understand. "What do you hunt with your knives?" I ask.

She frowns a little. "Other fighters. So that they may find their way out and I may find mine."

"You will die?"

She nods. "When I meet a fighter better than me. Better to die fighting than just wait for it. Only the weak ones wait for it."

There is a sound outside the door and she looks up sharply. "You'll tell me about the wolves later?" she asks and I nod.

"I'll see what we can do about getting food that's more like what you're used to," she is saying as the aide comes in the door. . . . I understand that he is not to know all of this. I understand that much, but no more.

She leaves and I am left with the aide. For a long time, even after the aide has dimmed the lights and is dozing in his chair, I stare up at the place where the wall meets the ceiling. A straight line, a hard edge in a world of confusion. I have much to learn.

I talk to the aides each day. I talk to James Andrews when he comes. I talk to strange men and women: other men and women called doctor, other men and women who ask many questions, other men and women I do not like and cannot trust. So many people.

I learn the most from talking with Zee each evening when the aide goes to dinner. I tell her about wolves and she tells me about the fights on the streets of the city. With her, I smoke cigarettes, a different way of smoking tobacco.

I tell her about my journey to see my people and about what the shaman told me—that I must learn and make peace with the bear.

The smoke curls away from the cigarette in her hand. She is leaning back in her chair, her legs stretched before her. "When I was tripping once, I went back to visit my mom. She's dead—been dead for years. It was nice. If I knew that I'd go back to my mom when I died, I wouldn't even wait to die in a fight." She shrugs. "But I don't know that. So I'll keep fighting." She blows another puff of smoke from between painted lips. "What'll you do if they won't send you back to the Valley to make peace with the bear?"

"I must go back to the Valley," I say.

"Yeah, but what if they won't send you?" I do not answer. "You could be a wolf like me," she says. "You'd be good." She leans forward a little and her mouth remains fixed in the same slight smile. "You have to understand—there's a power in it."

"The power to kill," I say.

"More than that," she says. Her eyes are steady. "The power to die. You'd be a good fighter."

This night, I dream of the bear. I often dream of the bear. In my dreams, she wanders the Valley, searching for me.

There are other nurses on some days and on some nights, but Zee is the only one who paints her face so brightly. Zee is the only one of my many visitors that I talk to so freely.

James Andrews talks to me in words that I do not understand. Usually, I watch the ceiling when he talks. I have stopped asking him when I will return to the Valley; he stopped answering before I stopped asking. "You don't seem to realize how important all this is," he says, in the dull voice that makes all the world seem unimportant. "Not only will the outcome of your case determine your own future, it will also set a precedent for the way that we deal with nonhuman species that prove intelligent." I stare at the ceiling. From what he has said before, I know that the Court and Moses will decide when I can return to the Valley. But I also know that what I say or do now can make little difference to the Court and Moses.

"We will be moving you soon," he says. "Away from the hospital and to a hotel. We'll have to make a decision—do you want an aide to stay with you in the hotel or . . ."

"I want to be alone," I say quickly.

"I don't know if that would be wise," he begins and he keeps talking, but I stop listening until he says, ". . . and then, the hearings before the Court will begin."

"Marshall will come to the hearings?" I ask. I have almost given up waiting for Marshall to come. Almost.

"Mr. Dustan has been delayed by a death in his family," Andrews says. "We expect that . . ."

I go back to staring at the ceiling and let his words run away in a babbling stream. Going nowhere.

That evening, Zee is not smiling when she brings my dinner. "You'll be leaving tomorrow," she says. "You'll be off and away. I won't be seeing you again." She sits silent for a moment. Zee is always a little cold, a little distant. She keeps the world away from her, always a little away. Then she shrugs and says easily, "Everything ends."

"Why won't you be seeing me again?"

"You're moving out, moving on into the world," she says. She stubs her cigarette in the ashtray and the cigarette breaks beneath her fingers. "I may see you. I'll wave from the back of the courtroom if they let me in."

I lie back in the bed. Everything ends, she said. This is something for me to learn. She puts the pack of cigarettes on the table beside my bed. "Here, you may need these until you find another sympathetic nurse. Bye, Sam." Her lips touch my cheek lightly and she is gone.

I do not sleep much that night.

Three aides and James Andrews come for me the next day and another nurse helps me dress in stiff clothing. I take the cigarettes from the table and put them in the pocket of the shirt. I do not like this room with its straight edges and flat walls. But at least I know these edges and these walls. I am not happy here, but I know this place. The door opens into a place that I do not know. I feel the way I felt when Amanda—*dark* led me out of my room at the Project.

The nurse gives me back my stone knife and the claws of the bear. With the knife in my pocket and the claws around my neck, I feel safer. I follow James Andrews and the aides. We walk through white corridors and step into a small room. A wall slides into place behind us.

"This is an elevator, Sam," one of the aides says.

I feel the room begin to move, though the walls stay just as they are. I can hear humming machinery all around us; I can hear my own heartbeat. There is nowhere to run.

The aide tells me not to worry, just to relax. I do not speak to him. At last, the room stops ... the elevator stops moving and the wall slides aside.

We walk into a world of cold stone and strange smells. This place is roofed—like an enormous cave—and filled with shiny things that I cannot name. "... underground garage," the aide is saying and his voice echoes. "These are cars." I can hear rumbling noises, like thunder in the distance. I can smell bitter smoke, like the smoke of Cynthia's snowmobile. I do not like this place. I want to run, but there is nowhere I can run.

The car is black and shiny and cold. It begins to growl, a steady sound that fills the place we sit. It begins to move, and I close my eyes against the shifting world around me.

The sound changes; the car stops, then moves again. "Hey, Sam," says the aide. He touches my shoulder lightly. "We're outside. You can open your eyes now."

The car has stopped again. I open my eyes. The sunlight is bright and, for a moment, the world is a blur of color moving around us. Bright, shifting colors— then I see clearly: people in bright clothing walking past the car; faces painted like Zee was painted, and faces that have no paint; so many people—more than are in my tribe, more than in all the tribes, more than in all of my world. Too many people.

They look toward me, but their eyes brush past mine as if they did not see. "It's one-way glass, Sam," says the aide who told me to open my eyes. "Relax. They can't see in."

I cannot relax. I did not know there were so many people in the world. Perhaps Amanda-*dark* is out there; I would not see her. I could not find her. So many people.

The people stop walking in front of the car and we move again, down long canyons between high cliffs. "Buildings," the aide names them. "Like giant houses, you know?" We follow a crooked path, but each time we stop there are people, more people.

The car turns down a hill and we go into darkness, as if into a cave. "Another garage," says the aide.

"We're almost there," says Andrews, who has sat silent the whole time. "Just a little farther to your room."

This elevator is larger and the floor is soft under our feet. The walls of the corridor are blue, like the sky. The lights are not bright, like they were in the hospital. There are golden balls, like small moons, that glow from the blue walls. The wall meets the ceiling in a curve, not a harsh line. This is a quiet place, after the rumble of the car.

A man waits for us in the corridor. He bends stiffly at the waist when he sees us. "So glad you will be gracing our hotel. . . ." he is saying and his voice is soft as rain on the hillside. ". . . manager, and if there is anything I can do to make your stay more pleasant, I hope that you will call on me." He bows again and Andrews nods back. The manager opens the door to the room.

This room is larger than the room at the hospital. There is a bed and a table and . . . other things. Andrews explains how the telephone works and how to "call room service." The TV is a screen like the one that Amanda—*dark* had at the Project, but the pictures the TV shows are not of my Valley. There are chairs, a sofa, a desk, and there is a bathroom as large as my room in the hospital. There is a window that looks down into a canyon where cars move. There are curtains to cover the window.

Andrews tells me that the hotel is secure, that if I need anything I must call room service, that this is a trial and if anything goes wrong he will have an aide stay with me. (I see the aide frown when he says this, but Andrews does not see.) And at last they say good-bye; many times, they say good-bye, and finally, they leave.

The room is quiet when they are gone. Quieter than the hospital where the sound of footsteps echoed from bare walls. At last, I am alone again and I am shivering now. Shaking like a fawn whose mother has been killed. I shiver and I cannot stop. There are too many people in this strange world. Too many. I take a blanket from the bed and I wrap it around myself, but still I shiver. This world is too big. After a while, after a long while, the shaking stops.

The shaman said that I must learn. I open the curtains and look out on the canyon filled with moving cars and people. I start to shiver again, looking out on the world that is too big, but I wrap the blanket around me and at last the shivering stops again. I wish that I had the hide of the old buck here, so I could dream of days past with my herd. This blanket has no memories.

But the shivering stops and I sit by the window, watching this strange world. Though I cannot see the sun, I know it must be setting. The light is fading. Soon, I cannot see the cars below. Instead, a stream of lights flows past, lights like fireflies. They move this way and that way, with as little sense as fireflies.

I light one of the cigarettes Zee gave me and I watch the lights. Now moving, now stopping. At the place where one canyon meets another, there is a light that does not move. It changes color as I watch— red, then green, then gold, then red. When it is red, the lights stop flowing in one direction and flow along the other canyon. When it turns green, the pattern shifts and the lights move in another way.

I blow out a puff of smoke and watch it curl up toward the ceiling. I can hear the cars rumbling below. There is a pattern to the way they move through the canyons.

In this world, the people come and the people go. Amanda—*dark,* Roy Morgan, Ben, Marshall, Zee—they come and they go and I am alone in a room high above a river of cars. But maybe there are reasons and maybe there are patterns that I cannot see. Maybe I can learn what the reasons are and how to follow the patterns. Maybe I can learn.

The cars stop and go. Spirit world or not, there are patterns here that I can learn and use, like a hunter uses the habits of his prey.

For a moment, as I watch the lights below, I am glad. I feel clean as though I have been in the sweathouse, then rolled in the snow. I feel as though I had returned from a quest for a vision, though I have gone nowhere. I am ready to met the bear, to talk to Moses and the court.

There is a sound at my door—a sharp knock on the wood. I frown, not knowing what to do. I go to the door and open it.

"I had to bribe three court aides and the hotel manager," Marshall says. He is pale and thin and he is grinning. "I just came back and they wouldn't tell me where you were hiding."

My shout echoes down the hall and I hug him. He is laughing. Still the bear claws dangle around his neck. Still he is taller than I am and his eyes are blue. And he is here; I can touch him; he is not a spirit.

"Came back from where?" I ask.

"From the moon," he says. "From the asteroid belt. From a long ways off."

We sit in the room, the curtains drawn now. We share a pipe and I tell him all that happened since he left the Valley.

He tells me that Ben decided to take him out to the Belt shortly after they returned from the Valley. He says he had only time to send the letter, not really thinking that it would do any good. "I didn't think that Moses would have anything to do with this," he says.

I say, "Many people have told me about Moses, but I still do not understand what Moses is."

"My dad used to say that Moses was going to change this world into another one—but no one could know what the new one would be like." Marshall stops. His face is stiff and I see that one of his hands is clutching the other.

"Where is Ben?" I ask carefully.

"He's dead," Marshall says softly. His face does not move and his hands do not move. "That's why I'm back. He wouldn't have let me come."

His face is stiff and he does not cry. He tells me of Ben's death, speaking in a steady voice. Ben died in an accident—not a major accident, just a faulty air lock and a defective suit, Marshall says. But the size of the accident did not matter. "You can die from a little accident out there," he says. "One minute, Ben was there. Then he was gone."

We sit and smoke together. I think of trying to tell Marshall about the patterns that I have seen in the canyon below, in the world around us. But I do not think that he wishes to learn of patterns now.

"And so I came back," Marshall says at last.

"I am glad you are home," I say, and he smiles just a little.

7

James Andrews is not happy to find Marshall sitting on my bed. We are eating the breakfast that room service sent to us. I am sitting on the floor, a more comfortable spot to sleep than the bed, I think. I am spreading butter on a bread thing that Marshall called an English muffin.

"What are you doing here?" Andrews asks Marshall.

"Eating breakfast," Marshall says with a slow smile. "I'm Marshall Dustan."

"Yes, Mr. Dustan, I recognize you. But I fail to see...." Andrews goes on talking, but I know from his unhappy expression that nothing will come of all his words. Marshall is at home in this world of the city and I watch the way he talks to Andrews, calmly butters a piece of toast, and smiles in certain ways.

"Of course," Marshall is saying. His tone is that of a young man speaking to a powerful shaman. "I understand the problems that my presence here may cause. But I'm Sam's blood brother and his friend and . . ."

He talks for a long time, Andrews talks for a long time and, eventually, Marshall talks longer than Andrews. Andrews shrugs and finally leaves.

The world moves more quickly, now that Marshall is here. Or maybe it is because I am out of the hospital, or because I am beginning to see the patterns of things. But the world moves more quickly.

We have something that Marshall calls a press conference. A press conference is a big room filled with people. Some people carry metal eyes that remind me of the eyes that I destroyed in the Valley. Some carry pads of paper and boxes that make a bright flash of light—Marshall calls the boxes and eyes both cameras. We go to the press conference in a car, but this time Marshall is at my side.

They ask me many questions. What do I think of this city? What are my impressions of cars? Of TV? Of Moses? Of women? How do I think that the trial will go? What do I think of Roy Morgan?

Marshall answers many of the questions. I answer some—saying, "I do not know. I have not met Moses. I do not watch the TV."

A press conference is too many people and too many questions but, eventually, it is over.

With Marshall, I go to breakfast in the hotel dining room. I go to lunch. I can see the many people (so many people) on the street (yes, I know this is a street now) without wanting to hide from so many people. Marshall stays in my room each night and I am glad he is here.

He goes with me to the Court when James Andrews takes me there. In the room that Andrews calls a courtroom there are many people. Roy Morgan is here; Cynthia sits beside him.

The people here are quiet, as if they are afraid to speak too loudly. There is not the ritual that comes with a judging in my Tribe. There is no chanting, no exchange of presents.

There is a man in black who sits at the front of the room. Beside him, there are seven empty seats. I know from Andrews that there are eight judges, and that they will come to the hearing on different days. Sometimes more than one will come. Sometimes, only one.

A camera, like the ones in the Valley, watches an empty seat beside the judges' chairs. A man sits beside the camera at a table filled with buttons and lights and dials. I watch him for a while, but I can see no sense in what he is doing.

Marshall sits on one side of me and Andrews sits on the other. And we listen to something that Andrews calls background information. Background information is small men with charts. They talk of costs and money and benefits and . . . all that I hear makes little sense to me. Background information is the doctor who visited me in the hospital. He talks of "voluntary starvation and exposure. . . ." Background information is a woman called a psychologist, a man called a linguist, the aides who were in my room when I woke up and many other men and women. There is a man who talks of cameras, a woman who talks of geographical redesign and many others.

Each day, we sit in the courtroom and we listen. Some days, one judge sits before us. Some days, there are two judges. Some days, three. I cannot tell how the rules to this Court work—sometimes one judge asks questions, sometimes Andrews stands and talks. But it is all very dull and very quiet.

At night, Marshall sleeps in my room and each night I dream of the bear. Always, I dream of the bear and the Valley.

During the day, I do not listen to the people who sit in what Andrews calls the witness stand. I watch the people who are in the courtroom. I watch Cynthia, who sits by Roy Morgan. Her face is cold and frozen; it never changes. Roy Morgan's face changes with the witnesses. Sometimes he turns to Cynthia and she speaks to him softly. He nods and smiles when she speaks to him.

In the back of the room, I see a tall man with a nose like a hawk's beak and long legs that he stretches under the chair in front of him. He looks toward the front of the room, but he seems to be looking beyond the judges and the witnesses.

I point him out to Marshall. "That's Dr. Karalekas," Marshall says. "He'll be testifying later."

On the day that is later, six judges sit at the front of the courtroom. Dr. Karalekas stalks to the witness stand with his hands hooked in his pockets and his eyes on the floor. He settles into the chair awkwardly and leans forward as if he will not sit for long.

"State your name, please," says one of the men who sits near the judges.

"Dr. Vincent Karalekas," he says.

"Your occupation, Dr. Karalekas?"

He runs one hand nervously through his hair. "Mathematician, more or less. Mathematician and some other things. Right now, I am directing the Outreach Project for the Morgan Foundation."

Marshall whispers to me that the Outreach is Roy Morgan's new project. He is trying to reach out to other planets, using the same methods that let him reach through time. I ask Marshall what a planet is, and he says that he will explain later. Andrews glares at us both and we are quiet.

"You have been employed by the Morgan Foundation for a period of five years," one judge is saying. "You were instrumental in the work on the time-travel project, isn't that so?"

The doctor shifts in his chair. He is not comfortable up in the witness stand. "That is so. It was based on my theories."

"Did you have any objections to the way that Mr. Morgan handled the project?"

Dr. Karalekas leans forward in his chair. He looks up at the judge, squinting against the light. "To work out the consequences of my formulas, I needed engineers and funding. Morgan gave me both. He understood what I wanted to do and he did not laugh. I had no objections." The doctor spreads his hands and shakes his head. "You have to understand, I was a crackpot. I was laughed at. But Morgan . . . he is an even bigger crackpot than I. He is a dreamer and dreamers are all crazy. All crazy." He shrugs. "This Outreach project . . . it's crazy too. It'll work, but it's crazy. But I had no objections to Morgan's kind of crazy."

A judge who has not spoken before leans forward to speak. "I have a very simple question, doctor. Can we send Sam back to his own time?"

The doctor leans forward, rubs one hand against the other, leans back, shifts his weight in the chair and looks even more unhappy. "No," he says. "I do not think we can."

"Why not?"

"We don't know enough about it yet. So far, we can yank things forward or throw them forward, but we can't send them back. We can only go in the natural direction." He stops and looks at me. "I wish we knew the way to send Sam back. I didn't mean to start something that would take someone from his own place. I'm sorry."

I want to tell him that he did not bring me here. The trickster spirit of the bear brought me. I start to stand, but Marshall's hand on my arm stops me. Karalekas does not look at me as he leaves the witness stand.

Other witnesses come and go that day, and that night I dream of the bear. The next day, all the seats at the front of the courtroom are filled; eight judges are there. And Roy Morgan goes to the witness stand.

I do not listen to his words always. I watch his face. He is controlling himself. He talks calmly of the Foundation and the Project. He talks of building the Valley—buying the land and redesigning the Valley for his needs. He talks of trying to build an ecosystem, bringing back species that would not interbreed, that could establish a balance. "We need to understand more about how to redesign a world," he says. "More about how to work with different ecological systems. When the Outreach succeeds . . ."

"Don't you mean 'If the Outreach succeeds'?" a judge interrupts.

Roy Morgan raises his eyebrows slightly. "I don't think the matter is in question. You'd have to ask Dr. Karalekas for a scientific opinion. But as I was saying . . ."

"He's smooth," Andrews whispers to an aide. "Tossing in the Outreach like that will push some in his favor. Very smooth."

"We did not mean to bring Sam here," Roy Morgan is saying. "We were bringing a cave bear, but Sam came too."

"Why didn't you bring this matter to the court's attention?" a judge asks. "This aspect of your work has . . ."

Roy Morgan loses his control for a moment. "You need to ask that? Now that my work is interrupted; the Project is on trial. . . ."

"This is not a trial, Mr. Morgan," the judge interrupts. "This is a hearing."

Morgan stops and his voice is controlled when he speaks again. "I spoke too hastily. I apologize." He pauses for a moment, then continues. "I felt the secrecy was in Sam's own best interest."

"You feel that Sam is best off in your charge?" another judge says. "You think he is incapable of living outside the Project?"

"Not incapable." Morgan hesitates and one of his

hands moves in the air, as if trying to grasp the right words. "You are accustomed to dealing in large problems, ones that affect the world. I was thinking of one man. Sam could live in this world of ours, without beasts to hunt, trapped in a world he does not understand. But he wouldn't like it." Now Morgan is speaking with power and the spirit of the hyena peers from his eyes. "I understand this because I built the Valley. There was nowhere left on this world to go. I know what we once had—game roamed Africa, great whales swam in the sea, my father and his father hunted in the Yukon, in Alaska. But all that is gone. So I built my own world. And that's Sam's world, too." He stops and his hands relax. "Ask Sam yourself if he will live in this outside world. The place he wants to be is the Valley. And the Valley is part of the Project."

"And since the Valley is yours, you feel that Sam must remain your charge," one judge says casually.

There is something happening here that I do not understand. Something swirls beneath the surface of their words like the eddies and whirlpools beneath the smooth surface of a river.

Roy Morgan glares at the judge. "Yes," he says sharply. "That's exactly it."

Andrews speaks softly to the aide who sits beside him. "Any attempt to nationalize that land would mean legislation at the Federal level. That won't happen. Morgan has too many friends."

"They're just teasing him," the aide says softly.

"I think the phrase is 'playing with him.' " The two men laugh softly.

More words from the judges, more from Roy Morgan, but the important part is over. I watch Morgan's face and the control is with him again. He does not look at me when he steps down from the stand. He sits beside Cynthia and I see her touch his arm and whisper. He nods, as if reassured.

"Marshall," says Andrews, and Marshall goes to the

stand and tells about his time in the Valley. He says nothing that I do not know. The eddies and whirlpools that swirl beneath the surface of the courtroom are still there, but they swirl around Marshall; they do not affect him.

Then Andrews says softly, "Sam," and it is my turn to speak before the Court and the camera.

The chair in the witness stand is soft. The judges look different, now that I am close to them. I can see them as separate people now—five old men and three old women, all dressed in black.

The lights are hot on my face and the camera watches me. Andrews told me once that the camera made a record of the hearing and that information from that record was given to Moses. I look at the camera now that I am near it, but it looks like all the metal eyes that I destroyed in my Valley.

"Hello, Sam," says one judge. "We'd like you to tell about what has happened to you since you left your tribe."

"Yes," I say. When I speak, my voice booms back at me from the room and I look around, startled.

"That's the microphone, Sam. Try to ignore it. Just tell us your story, in your own words."

I nod. The room is silent.

"On a night long ago, I dreamed of the bear," I say. My voice booms back at me, but I ignore it. I tell the tale as I told it to my tribe. "The grass was long and green and the air was warm with the sunlight of spring. I went to hunt the bear." I watch the faces of the judges and the eye of the camera. When I tell of Roy Morgan and Amanda—*dark,* I see that some judges are watching Roy Morgan. I tell of how Amanda—*dark* went away; I tell of my hunt with Marshall and I tell of the bear spirit who wanders the Valley. One woman frowns when I speak of waiting by the cave of the bear and a man shakes his head when I tell of my return to my tribe. I tell of the shaman and of how he told me I must make my peace with the bear.

"And so I am here," I say. "And I know that I must go back to the Valley. The bear is waiting for me. I dream of her spirit and I know I must go back."

I stop and the room is silent for a moment.

"Suppose you could not go back to the Valley?" asks the woman who frowned. She is still frowning.

"I must go back," I say. "The bear is waiting for me."

"But what if you could not go back?"

I do not know what to say. I look out over the room and I can see Marshall in the front row. I can see Roy Morgan and Cynthia, side by side. And in the back of the room, for the first time, I see Zee, smiling as she watches me. She is dressed in black and red, and her lips and eyes are painted brighter than they ever were at the hospital. Her arms are folded across her chest and she is grinning at me. She asked me the same question and suggested an answer.

No one sits in the chairs to either side of her. Her legs are stretched out in front of her, into the gap between groups of chairs, and I can see the glint of a knife, strapped to her leg.

"I do not know what it means to die in this world," I say. "I could not join my tribe until I make peace with the bear." I hesitate. "But there would be no other way."

The judge is frowning. "You could live in this world."

"No," I say. "I cannot live here." And then, because I am done talking, I stand and I go back to my seat beside Marshall. Andrews is scowling and shaking his head and the judge calls for me to come back, but I cross my arms over my chest. "I have said all that I have to say," I tell Andrews and I only shake my head when he talks to me. At last, he goes up to the place the judges sit and talks with them quietly. I look to the back of the room, but Zee is gone.

And that is all. The judges leave and then we all go back to the hotel. Andrews is unhappy with me and complains about the way I acted, but Andrews is always unhappy. Marshall says that we must wait now for a decision and we wait. We eat dinner in the hotel dining room and outside the window, people hurry past. Marshall sleeps in my room and I dream of the bear.

We wait and we do not go to the courtroom the next day. Marshall takes me on a tour of the city. It is filled with people I do not know, hurrying to places that I do not understand. He takes me to a place he calls the Park.

Here, there are trees and grass but the trees do not smell like trees and there are no deer to crop the grass.

Marshall takes me to the Zoo, and I remember that Zee said there were wolves here. The beasts stand behind moats and sometimes behind bars. The cages are cleverly made to seem large and open.

"This is one of the largest zoos in the world," Marshall says. "They've bred a number of endangered species here, animals that don't live in the wild anymore."

I look across a moat at a bull bison who stares back at me. His hump is larger and his head is bigger than those of bison that my tribe hunted, but I know him. He has a strong spirit. Dust clings to his shaggy fur and he watches me with dark eyes.

"They have kept alive species of animals that would have been wiped out by now," Marshall says.

The bison stares at me across the moat and shakes his head.

"Why?" I ask Marshall.

Marshall frowns. "Because otherwise they would have died off."

I lean on the railing that separates us from the bison. "There is a strength in death," I say. "There is a dignity in death." I do not look at Marshall. I watch the bull lower his head to nuzzle at one hoof. "I am

102

the last of my people in this world," I say. "Must I live here just because I am the last? Though there is nowhere for me to go?" I look at Marshall then. His hands are gripping the rail. "Everything dies," I say. "Everyone dies."

"So you meant it," he says. "You meant it when you said that you would die if you did not go back to the Valley. I didn't want to ask, but . . ." He stops for a moment. "I didn't want to ask."

"I cannot live here," I say. "I do not know what death means in this world of yours." I shrug. "I do not know where it would take me, but I know I would go."

Marshall is watching the bull now. His face is set, tense, and his eyes are bright. "I don't know what death means," he says. "Ben is dead and I don't know what that means. It means I don't see him anymore, it means I run the company, but I don't know what it means. I still wonder what he would think of what I am doing." Marshall does not move. His hands are quiet on the rail. "I still wonder about whether he was careless with his suit and didn't check it carefully. I still wonder if he was careless because I was along and he checked my suit instead, or . . ." He stops talking suddenly. "Sam, if you die here, I would wonder if it was my fault for hunting with you, or for writing to the Court or . . ."

I put my hands on his two shoulders. He is confused and I do not understand why he is confused. It is a simple thing, death. Everything dies. "I will think well of you when I die," I say, but that does not seem to be enough.

When I embrace him, the bear claws on my neck rattle against the claws around his neck. "I will think well of you," I say again. It is not enough, but it is all I can say. I do not understand him; I do not understand these people.

*   *   *

This night, I do not dream of the bear.

I dream that I am in a room and I am alone. I sit in a chair, like the seat in the witness stand, and I know that I am in the courtroom. The room is filled with shadows. The eye that is the camera watches me. The air here is too warm. I do not belong here.

I am ready to jump at the smallest sound, just like Marshall was in my world. I do not belong here; this is not my dream. Yet is has the feel of a true dream.

"Sam?" says a voice that comes from everywhere.

The shadows are all around me. The shadows are everywhere. I do not know where to run. "Who are you?"

"I am Moses," says the voice. It is a deep voice, yet sweeter than a man's voice would be. It carries a note—not of pride—of acceptance.

I hesitate, frowning. "What are you, Moses? You are not beast, you are not human."

"I am Moses," the voice says again. "I am the only one of my kind."

"What do you want?" I ask.

"To ask questions," the voice says. "To find answers. I look for patterns in the world and I learn."

"I look for patterns," I say. "The shaman told me to learn."

"Yes," Moses says. "You see different patterns than I would see. Different patterns than the scientists would find. That is why I brought you out of the Valley and why I will send you back to the Valley. You fit into patterns and make different patterns and change patterns."

"I will go back to the Valley?" I say eagerly.

"For a while," Moses says. The voice is silent for a moment.

"Why am I here in this place?" I say, tapping my hand against the arm of the chair. "Why am I in this dream?"

"I brought you here," says Moses. The voice is

thoughtful. "I wanted to see if you would talk to me, and know that I am here and I am alive and I have a will and a spirit." The voice is fading. "The people who made me do not know these things. They don't know." The voice is gone and the dream is gone.

I awaken and wish that I could talk to the shaman and learn the meaning of this dream.

I tell Marshall of the dream over breakfast. He shakes his head. "It's just a dream, Sam. A screwy one, if you ask me. But only a dream."

That day, we go to court.

No one goes to the witness stand this day. The woman judge who frowned when I spoke is speaking now, and her words roll out like thunder in the mountains. The people sit quietly. Cynthia is at Roy Morgan's side. Her face is still, like a carving in ice. But her eyes are restless, shifting from Roy Morgan's face, to the judge's face, to the faces of the men working the cameras and writing in notebooks. The courtroom is more crowded today than it ever has been before.

Roy Morgan watches the judge. His face is steady—like the face of a man who knows what to expect. His arms are folded across his chest and he does not shift in his chair, though the judge is talking for a long time.

". . . recognize the problems inherent in this situation," the judge is saying. ". . . and also recognize the importance of this precedent . . ."

I can see Dr. Karalekas in the back of the courtroom. He is watching Roy Morgan, just as I am watching him.

". . . Sam, the Neanderthal," the judge is saying, "is to serve as caretaker in the Valley that he claims as his own. During his life, he is to control access to and treatment of these lands, though title is held by Morgan Foundation. Following his death, these rights revert. . . ."

I am not listening. I am watching Roy Morgan turn to Cynthia. I am watching Cynthia, her face still cold but her eyes wide in shock.

105

And the judge is saying, "This ruling is supported by the recommendations of Moses, of the Court Council, of . . ."

I cannot hear the rest. Marshall is patting me on the back and Andrews is talking with his aide and the men with cameras are holding them high and lights are flashing—on Roy Morgan, on Cynthia, on the judges, on me. And there is confusion for a time. The man who sits beside the judges bangs on a table for a while and eventually the room is quiet again. The judge finishes her words and it is all over.

For a moment.

Noise, confusion, lights flashing—it is as bad as the first press conference, though I am more used to the noise and confusion of this place. Roy Morgan is hidden by a crowd of people and Marshall keeps his hand firmly on my shoulder and pushes away microphones and the people who hold them. Andrews and his aide help clear the way. It is like walking up a river against the current.

"No statement now," Marshall is saying. "Nothing to say at this time. No comment." And we are trapped for a moment in an eddy, in a whirlpool in the crowd.

I look back. Roy Morgan is standing on a chair, shouting at the knot of people who surround him. I cannot hear what he is saying. The crowd parts for a moment and I can see Cynthia then. She is looking toward me, and her face is set in an expression that I have not seen on it before: she is afraid.

"You change the patterns," Moses had told me. Cynthia is starting to understand what I tried to tell her in the Valley. This is not the future she expected. I am here; I am changing the patterns of the future.

Then the people swirl around her and she is gone.

8

"You want to go back right away?" Marshall asks, though I have already told him twice that I must go back to the Valley now. "I thought you might want to stay and learn about this world before you go back. Just for a while. I could show you. . . ."

"I need to go back. The bear is waiting for me," I say. I lean back in the soft chair and look around the hotel room. I have grown used to this place, but I could never belong here. "I must go back," I say again.

Marshall starts to speak, stops himself, and sits silent for a moment.

"Marshall, my brother, I know you do not believe that the bear is real," I say. "But I must go back."

He frowns but nods. "All right. As soon as Andrews can set it up, we'll take you back." He leans back in his chair, but still he is frowning.

"What is it?" I ask him.

His frown deepens. "Roy Morgan left a message for you at the hotel desk," he says. "He wants to talk to you." Marshall does not give me time to speak; he leans forward with his hands on his knees. "You don't have to talk to him. He has no control over you now."

I stand and turn away from him, toward the window. Outside, night has fallen and the cars below move in patterns that have become familiar. Roy Morgan has no power over me now. I do not have to talk to him.

"I will talk to him," I say, watching the cars below.

"Why?" Marshall says. "It isn't necessary."

I shrug. In the true dream, Moses said that I changed the patterns of the world. Roy Morgan is powerful; I know that he, too, makes the patterns shift and change.

"I'll go with you," Marshall says. He wants to protect me though he does not know how.

On the next afternoon, we go to see Roy Morgan at the Morgan Foundation. The Foundation is outside the city and we drive down winding roads to reach it. Marshall does not talk much on the long drive; I know that he does not like coming here.

We stop at a set of stone gates to speak with a guard, then follow a long drive to the steps of the building. A woman dressed in a white lab coat, like Amanda—*dark* used to wear, meets us at the door and takes us to Roy Morgan's office.

Roy Morgan looks up from the papers at his desk when the woman waves us into his office and closes the door behind us. It is a strange thing to be at the Project again and to have a door closing at my back. It is strange, but Marshall is at my side. I meet Roy Morgan's eyes and for a moment I am startled. This is a different man than the man who came to see me in the Valley. Different from the man who met me in a room before I knew it was a room.

"Hello," he says. "I'm glad you came. Sit down." He gestures to two chairs before the desk. "Would you like something to drink? No?" He settles behind the desk.

The window behind him looks out over a wide, green lawn. It is late afternoon and the trees cast shadows across the grass—long, dark shadows. The shadows and the green grass remind me of the Valley at sunset, even though this is just a wide, green lawn on the Outside. It is not like the Valley at all.

Roy Morgan follows my gaze and smiles, just a little. "Tired of the city?" he says.

This is a different man than the man who spoke in the Court. I do not know this man. His eyes are not empty; his hands are quiet on his desk.

"Yes," I say. "I am going back to my Valley."

"I'll miss the Valley," he says. I tense when he says it, but he says it quietly and says no more about it. "And you, Marshall?"

"I will be carrying on my dad's business," Marshall says, and his voice is small and tight.

"Of course," Morgan says in a softer voice. I see something in his eyes that was not there before. Pity? Sorrow? "You know, I miss him too. Ben was a good friend."

Marshall barely nods.

Morgan is watching him, but Marshall does not look up. "I'm sorry that you dislike me," Morgan says. Marshall's head jerks up and he meets Morgan's eyes. "I know you do, but I don't know why." Morgan gazes at Marshall and Marshall is the first to look away.

Morgan shifts his gaze to me. Yes, this is a different man. He walks more softly. He is more careful. He would hunt well, I think.

"Now Sam has a reason to hate me," he says. "I brought him here."

I frown at him. He claims too much power for himself. "You did not bring me here," I say.

"No? Then who did?"

I am studying his face—still arrogant, but different now. "Amanda–*dark* brought me. The bear brought me. You did not."

"Ah," he says. "But you hate me. Why is that?"

"You made Amanda–*dark* leave."

His eyes are troubled now, not cold and distant. He shakes his head slowly. "I would have made her leave the Project," he says. "That's true. I was different then. I needed to test my own strength. But now, if she came back I would be glad to see her." He stops for a moment, looking down at his empty hands on the

109

desk. When he looks up, he is frowning, a little puzzled. "Everything's different now. I wish I could call Amanda–*dark* back. But I don't even know where she went."

I believe him. I believe he would call her back. He is not the same man. The hyena spirit is changing him. The spirit fills the hollow place that I sensed in him. "Cynthia threw Amanda–*dark* into another time," I say to him. "Into the future."

"Ah," he says, and his eyes are cold again.

"You say you'd call Amanda–*dark* back," Marshall interrupts. "Would you feel the same way if you had won in Court?" Marshall asks. His voice is harsh.

"I think so," Morgan says. "I can't know for sure." He studies Marshall's face, his tense shoulders, his clenched fists. "I think so."

"And what do you want from me?" I ask Morgan.

"I wanted to be your friend once," he says. "I still want that. But I also want to give you something." He leans forward in his chair and keeps his eyes on mine. "You heard of the Outreach in Court," he says. "We are reaching out to other worlds. We will find a world with beasts to hunt and wide green valleys. We will do it—just as we brought you here. And when we do, I will go to that new world. I can take you with me." His voice is low and filled with excitement. "A new world."

I have no use for a new world. I look past him to the green lawn where the dark shadows lie and I think of my Valley. I must make my peace with the bear; I must learn the ways of power. I need my own world, not a new one. I do not know why Morgan would want me in his new world.

"Why would you do that?" Marshall asks Morgan. "Out of friendship?" And he twists the last word so the sound is wrong.

Morgan's voice is strong when he speaks, and the hyena looks out of his eyes. "We will need Sam then.

110

We need him now." His eyes are bright and cold when he looks at me. "Now, you'll go to the Valley. Later, we'll talk again. Then, I will have a world to show you."

He is different, but I do not trust this man. I do not trust the spirit that looks from his eyes.

I stand to leave and Marshall stands with me. "Good luck, Sam," Morgan says. "Good luck to you both."

The woman in white takes us back to the door. We step out of the white corridor into the drive. Twilight has come to this world and the air smells of coming rain.

"He's smooth," Marshall says as we walk toward the car. "Real smooth. Talking about his good friend, Ben. You wouldn't go with him, would you?"

"I don't know."

"If you want to go to a new world, come with me to the Belt," Marshall says, and he shakes his head. "I'll never trust Morgan."

I do not say all that I think. I think that Morgan is stronger now. In his strength, he reminds me of Ben. But I do not speak of this to Marshall.

A pale figure waits for us by the car. She looks up when we come near, and I think that she is ready to run, to flee like a startled deer. Cynthia is thinner than she was. Dark shadows mark the pale skin under her eyes. Like Roy Morgan, she has changed. "Hello, Sam," she says, and her voice is soft. The icicles are gone from her words. She is afraid.

"Hello," I say. Marshall stands silent at my side and I study this woman. I do not fear her now; she cannot harm me.

"Things are changing," she says abruptly.

I frown, a little puzzled. "Yes. That is so."

She wets her pale lips and tries again. "Things are changing and I don't know what will happen." She stops again, as though she did not know how to continue. Her eyes flicker to Marshall's face, then back to mine. "Roy Morgan is different now. I don't understand."

"I told you once that there are powers that you don't understand," I say. "You did not believe me then. You said that everything would happen as you said."

"Why did you win at the Trial?" she says. Her voice holds a note of desperation. "You weren't supposed to. It was supposed to go for Morgan. I saw. . . ."

"Moses changed that," I say softly, realizing only now that this is so. The large spirit that spoke to me in a dream gave me the Valley. "He helped them decide my way."

"Moses? Moses is a big computer system; Moses pushes data around and pushes out answers. It's just a way of manipulating data. . . ."

"No," I say. "Moses is a strong spirit, made by your people." How is it that these people do not even know the spirits that they create? "He is . . ."

"No," she cries. "No, he's just . . . it's just a machine. That's all."

"You do not understand this world," I say. "You do not understand all that is here. You do not know the power that has touched Roy Morgan."

"Do you understand?" she asks in a shrill voice. "Do you know the way?" Her pale hands grip each other.

I shake my head.

"You don't know." She is glad and spiteful. "You don't know, either."

Marshall moves restlessly at my side. "No one knows, lady," he says. "Hey, Sam, we'd better get going. I mean, we should head back. . . ."

"Yes," I say. But I do not move. I look at the pale woman in the twilight and I ask the question that I have been wanting to ask. "Cynthia, will you tell me? When will I see Amanda—*dark* again?"

Her spiteful smile widens. "I don't know. I threw her forward and I thought I knew when she would be back. But I don't know anymore. The world is changing and I can't see. . . ." Something cold breaks behind her smile and she bows her head. Her pale hands cover her staring eyes.

When she looks up again, her eyes are empty. She turns abruptly, running back to the building where no one is waiting for her. We go then, driving down the winding road into the deepening twilight.

It is time to go back to the Valley, but not yet time. I must learn to write my name and write it on many papers for James Andrews. I must have a press conference. And I must wait.

Marshall gives me things that he says I must take to the Valley; a metal pot, a metal cup, a cook stove, a hatchet, a pack to carry them all. I take these things only because they are Marshall's gifts. I do not need them.

Soon, but not soon enough, we drive a car to the place Marshall calls the airport. We fly in a machine called a plane and, though it is strange and frightening, it is not important. I care only about going back to my Valley.

We drive again, Marshall, Andrews and I. The mountains here look familiar. It is midsummer and the fields are green, touched with flowers. Andrews follows many winding roads. At last, he stops the car at a marker. "I'll wait here," he says.

Marshall walks with me, showing me the way. "I'll be back in a month or so," he says. "We'll set up a radio hookup so you can get in touch. And . . ."

But I am not listening. I know this hill. I could see it through the Barrier when I was in the Valley.

"Listen to me, Sam," Marshall is saying. "You'll need to know this." We have stopped at the top of the hill beside a gray tooth that I recognize. I can see the line of gray teeth stretching away into the distance.

Marshall gives me a gray box that he says will

cancel out the field of the Barrier and he explains how it works, but I am not listening.

"Good-bye," I say finally.

"See you soon, Sam," he says. "See you. . . ."

I step through the Barrier and I am back in my Valley. I have come back to the Valley of the bear.

9

The Valley has not changed.

I follow the old path down the rocky slope to the Valley floor. The wind is sweet and cool and it carries the scents of autumn. Summer passed while I was on the Outside and the grass in the Valley is dried to a golden brown.

My hut stands, just as I left it. The dried meat that I hung in the hut has been gnawed by small beasts; my stores of berries have been stolen by birds and beasts. But the hut is there. Still the spring bubbles with clear water. Still the stream runs along the edge of the meadow.

This evening, I sit on the flat rock in the meadow and my world flows around me. I watch the deer grazing on the far side of the Valley. I can hear the wild swine in the brush by the stream. The insects in the grass cry in a steady rhythm.

The Valley has not changed. I have changed. I was young and afraid when I left my Valley. I am young still, but I am not afraid now.

The shadows stretch and darken. The red glow fades

to gray twilight, and still I sit on the flat rock, listening to the insects cry in the grass. I hear a sound—a low growl. I catch the scent of the bear on the twilight wind.

I see the gray shadow of the she-bear spirit, standing in the meadow grass a stone's throw from me. She is watching me and I meet her gaze. She does not move and I do not move. She is watching me, only watching me. She shifts her weight from one foot to the other, swaying a little, but she does not move toward me. She is watching me.

"I have come back," I say to her in the Old Tongue. "There must be peace between us."

Then the meadow is empty and I am speaking to the darkness. The wind carries only the scent of swine and deer and the sound of singing insects. She is gone for now.

This night, I sleep under the rock ledge, wrapped in my old deerskin. I sleep uneasily, awakening at the sounds of small beasts prowling in the night. Once, I catch the scent of the she-bear on the wind, but the wind shifts and the scent is gone. My dreams are empty.

I awaken at dawn and I begin as I must begin. I have grown soft during my days on the Outside. Now I hunt. I run down a boar and kill him with spear and knife. His flesh and his spirit make me strong. I run in the meadow to make my body stronger. I rebuild the sweathouse and I sweat the scents and tastes of the Outside from my body. I grow stronger.

Sometimes, on the night wind, I smell the she-bear. Sometimes, in the twilight, I hear a sound that could be her growling. But I do not see her. I feel tension in the air, like the feeling before a thunderstorm. I know that she is waiting, but she does not come to me. I do not know how to call her, but I think that I must learn.

On a sunny day, a week from the day that I returned

115

to the Valley, I go to the cave of the bear. I climb the mountain slope, glad to have the rock beneath my feet and the blue sky over my head. I have left the clothes that Marshall gave me back at the hut, and the autumn wind blows on my skin.

I pick my way carefully through the rocks to reach the place where the bear fell. The smell of death is gone; only the bones remain. I do not know why I have come to this place. I do not know what I expect to find.

Hungry beasts have scattered the she-bear's bones. Hyenas have crushed and broken some; foxes and other beasts have left the marks of their teeth on others. The rocky slope is exposed to the sun and the bones that lie here are beginning to crack and whiten.

A jumble of bones is caught in a crack between two rocks. I squat to look more closely. The bones are from the bear's paw and forearm. They are still bound to each other, though the skin and hair is falling away in tatters. I can see where I cut the claws free.

I reach out to touch the whitening bone. At my touch, the bones fall apart. I am left holding three flattened knucklebones—bones that match the claws dangling around my neck.

The sun shines on the back of my neck and warms me. The rock beneath my feet is warm and I feel like I belong here; I am a part of the mountain. I turn the bones over and over in my hand. They have fallen into my hand as if they belonged to me.

The way of power has chosen me. The old shaman told me that in my true dream. It is not a question of wanting or asking.

I am to be a shaman, and so I must gather the tools of a shaman. I must make them as a hunter makes his weapons. A hunter would not chase a deer without knife and spear. A shaman would not journey in the world of the spirits without his tools of power: his drum, his bones, his herbs.

The shaman of my tribe could tell the will of the spirits by throwing the bones. I will take these bones and I will begin to learn the ways of the shaman. I stand and I slip the three bones into the pouch at my side.

The skull of the bear stares at me from beneath a rock ledge. Her eye sockets are empty, but still she is watching me.

"Will you speak to me, Great One?" I say to the skull. "Will you come out and speak to me? It is time that there was peace between us."

I take a step toward the skull. My leg is stiff from its injury last winter, but I stand firm and proud. "Will you come to me?" I ask her.

Above my head, I hear a coughing grunt. I look up, and another set of eyes is watching me. A she-bear—younger than the bear that Marshall killed—is watching me from the ledge beside the cave. She shakes her head at me and coughs again, a warning sound that tells me to go now and go quickly.

I step back from the skull slowly. "We will meet soon, Great One," I say softly. The bear growls and I back away, leaving the skull and the bones behind.

I return to my Valley. I do not know how to call the bear spirit to me. But if I am to be a shaman and a man of power, I must learn. A young man who wants to be a shaman must find a shaman to help him. But there is no shaman here, and I must learn as well as I can.

On this next day, I sit on the flat rock in the meadow. The sun shines on me and far away, a herd of deer grazes.

I smooth the knucklebones that I took from the bear, rubbing them against the flat rock to wear the edges smooth. I work slowly. I will mark one side of each by scratching it with a deep notch, and then I will have bones like the shaman's bones.

I did not hear the bear last night. But now I can feel

117

tension in the air, just as I can smell the pines on the wind. I am less sure now that I can learn to call the spirit, less sure that I can learn to be a shaman with no shaman to guide me. The mountains rise around me and I feel small and alone.

I had grown used to being with Marshall. I had forgotten how it was to be alone, always alone. I did not belong on the Outside, but I do not like to be alone.

The wind shifts and carries the scent of deer to me. I look up and the herd of deer is closer. They are grazing quietly. A young buck lifts his head and meets my eyes. I know him—he is son of the buck I killed long ago. He is my son. This is my herd.

They step softly through the grass, still grazing as they surround the flat rock. They accept me; I belong with them. A young doe grazes beside the rock, her young daughter at her side. The doe does not move to stand between her daughter and me. Right now, I am not a hunter. We are part of the same herd.

The herd moves around me and I feel the spirit of the buck within me. I feel strong. The young buck who is my son tosses his head to catch my gaze. When he sees that I am watching, he lowers his head and brushes his muzzle against a plant that grows beside the rock. He stamps his foot beside the plant—one, two, three times.

When he looks up at me, his eyes are not those of my son, not those of a young buck. His eyes are bright and hard and wise, and he looks at me as if he were measuring me, judging me. He tosses his head again and his eyes change. He is only a young buck, grazing with the herd. The herd moves away and he moves with them. I watch them go.

I break a leaf from the plant he nuzzled and the sap is sticky on my hands. I do not like the smell of the plant's white, horn-shaped flowers. The scent is heavy and sweet and it reminds me of the scent of the drink the shaman makes. The shaman's drink made him see clearly in the world of the spirits. I need to see clearly in the world of the spirits. I do not like this plant, but soon I will use it.

I am not yet ready. Before I journey in the world of the spirits, I need a drum. Each shaman has a drum. The sound of the drum's steady beat guides him to the spirit world and back to his own world again. I will make a drum, and then perhaps I will be ready. I must be ready to meet the spirit who looked at me through the eyes of the buck.

This night, I dream of the buck with wise eyes. He dances around my hut as I sleep and I do not hear the bear prowling in the night. I call out to the buck, but he does not stop dancing or speak to me. The insects cry in the night and he dances to their song. He is older now, this buck, and his antlers reach to the sky. I know that my time to journey is soon.

At dawn, I go to the side of the mountain, where I remember a gnarled and ancient tree. This tree was struck by lightning long ago—touched by power from the sky. Still it grows—but one, thick branch is dead. I take this branch from the tree, chopping it free with the hatchet that Marshall gave me. It would be better to burn it free, using the power of fire on a tree that has been touched with fire. But I know that the time is coming for me to journey and I must hurry.

On the flat rock, I build a hot fire. With flaming brands, I burn out the center of the log. This is slow work—I burn some and scrape away the charred wood, then burn again. I stop when the sun is low to run in the meadow and check my snares for rabbits. I eat a little, drink clear water from the spring, then go back to the log and the fire. I sleep beneath the rock ledge and dream of the buck with wise eyes. In the dream, I beat the drum and the buck dances to my music. In his mouth, the buck carries a branch of the shaman's plant, plucked from beside the rock. The white flowers

119

seem to glow in the moonlight and I know the time is coming.

The dawn is cool and clear and there is a tension in the air. The wind carries the scent of coming rain. I go to the flat rock and take leaves and branches from the shaman's plant. I crush them—as I remember seeing the shaman crush plants for medicinal brews. I put the leaves in a pot that Marshall gave me, and I fill the pot with clear spring water. I set the pot on the flat rock, where the sunlight will warm it so that the water can take the magic from the plant.

I sit in the sunshine on the flat rock and I make a drum skin from part of the skin of the first buck I killed. With a needle of bone, I make holes in the drum skin. I lace sinew through the holes to bind the skin to the log.

The time has almost come. The water in the pot is a pale green and I can smell the heavy, sweet scent of the plant. I tap on the drum and the sound is solid and good. But I tighten the sinew and tap the skin again—a solid sound echoes across the Valley.

A shadow falls on me. A dark cloud has covered the sun and the wind blows cold. The air is filled with tension and power. The mountains seem taller than they once did. The time is here.

I take the pot in both my hands. The drink is still warm from the sun; it tastes of leaves and greenery—little more. Carefully, I set the bowl back on the rock.

The world around me is waiting. The insects have stopped singing in the grass. The sky has grown darker. The Valley is waiting.

I beat my drum and I begin to chant softly in the Old Tongue. I do not know the proper chant for a shaman, but I make my own words. "I am looking . . . I am looking for the way. . . ."

Though the sky is dark, the colors in the Valley seem bright, so bright I must squint my eyes against them. A sharp pain comes to me then; my stomach

120

twists within me. But I do not stop chanting. The pain passes, then comes again—like a twisting and pulling on my stomach. The ground is not steady beneath me; it moves and shifts like water.

"I am seeking . . . I am seeking out the way. . . ." I chant. The thunder answers my chant. It rolls over the mountains from far away, rumbling and crashing like a tremendous drum. Rain falls—a few drops at first. Then sheets of gray rain sweep over the mountains and beat against the grass of the meadow. The rain is cold on my back; it beats against my hands.

"I am waiting . . . I am waiting for the way. . . ." Though my eyes are half closed, the colors are still bright—too bright. I am not seeing them with my eyes and I cannot shut them out. Yellows as bright as the sun; reds like the bright blood of a new kill; green like new grass—all bright, bright enough to burn me. My throat is tight, but I chant and I beat my drum.

"I am going . . . I am going far away. . . ." A shadow, shifting in the rain, seems to be dancing to my drumbeat and to the beat of the thunder. The she-bear shuffles toward me, a dancing shadow in the rain. She glares at me with reddened eyes and circles me, dancing to the beat of the rain and the thunder. It is the rain that called her. I know that I could not call this one to me. It is the wind that blew her to this place.

"I am going . . . I am going on my way. . . ." The world is darker around me and the wind is stronger. The wind and the thunder are part of my music and I cannot feel the rain on my skin. The bear dances, and the silver sheen of her fur grows brighter each time she circles, shimmering as though she danced in the moonlight.

The wind blows darkness around me and there are no stars. No stars and I find that I am walking in the darkness, still beating my drum. I cannot feel my feet as they touch the ground. I know this place—this is the place the old shaman and I said good-bye.

I beat the drum as I walk. I know, though I do not know how, that I must beat the drum and I must chant, or the bear will not dance and I cannot follow her. "I am walking . . . I am walking on the way. . . ." The bear glances back at me with angry eyes and still I follow. This is a cold world and the wind steals my heat from me, but still I drum.

The darkness ahead is spotted with lights—no, not lights. Eyes. A pack of dire-wolves waits for us, each animal's yellow eyes gleaming in the darkness. The leader of the pack is larger than any wolf I have ever seen. He stands and grins when he sees me and his eyes are hard and bright, like the eyes of the buck.

I beat a steady rhythm on my drum and I chant in time. The bear dances through the center of the pack and I follow. I can feel the hot breath of the wolves on my legs, but I do not stop chanting. I follow the bear.

We walk through a place where snakes squirm on the ground and hiss as we pass. The largest snake coils and lifts his head to watch us. His eyes are wise and cold.

We walk through a herd of mammoth and the old bull that leads them stares at me with considering eyes. But I do not stop drumming. I follow the bear.

We climb a mountain slope, toward a light that shines as steadily as the moon. "We are coming," I chant. "We are coming on the way. . . ."

A man waits for me in the light at the mountaintop.

No, not a man. Antlers rise from his head; a tail, like a lion's tail, sweeps the ground behind him. He stands on hooves and his legs are as shaggy as the legs of the bison. His hands are tipped with claws like the claws of a cat.

He stares at me and I recognize the look in his eyes. He was the spirit in the young buck; he was the leader of the wolf pack; he was the snake and the mammoth. When he looks at me, my chant dies in my throat. My hands stop tapping on the drum.

122

Suddenly, I do not feel as strong as I once felt.

The she-bear stands beside him. She has reared up on her hind legs and her fur is silver in the strange light of this place. She growls—a rumbling like the thunder—and I can hear words in her growling. "No good," she is rumbling in the Old Tongue. "He is a fool. He fears me and he fears you and . . ."

He turns to glare at the she-bear and she stops growling. He turns back to look at me, and his tail twitches impatiently.

"Are you afraid?" he asks.

I must tell him what is so, for he would know if I spoke less than the truth. "I am afraid," I say. When I speak, my voice is rough from chanting.

"Then he is not a fool," he says to the bear.

The she-bear shakes her heavy head and glares at me with her red-rimmed eyes. She does not speak again in her growling voice.

"Do you know who I am?" he asks me.

I know him—from tales that the shaman told long ago. I know him by the beasts who serve him. He is Master of the Beasts and Master of the Hunt. "You are the Animal Master," I say. "The beasts we hunt are yours."

He nods slowly, watching me closely. "Do you know why you are here?" he asks.

I keep my eyes on his. Beside him, the she-bear is shuffling her feet and swaying from side to side. She is restless, angry, and I do not look at her. "I wish to make peace with the bear," I say. "It is not finished between us."

"That is why you came here," he says. "That is not why I showed you the way. You must understand that as well." His eyes have not moved from mine—he is studying me and judging me. "For a moment, you must watch. I will show you something that will help you understand."

He waves a paw in the air and the wind swirls dark

123

around us. Darker, darker . . . and I can see only the Animal Master's face. I hear a voice, speaking in the Old Tongue.

The darkness clears and I see a man, speaking to the Animal Master. The man is not aware of me; he is speaking to the Animal Master. "I have come to you for my people," he is saying.

The man wears a shaman's pouch at his side, but it is woven from river reeds, not sewn from hide. He is thin, this shaman. He wears no hides and he shivers in the wind. But he looks up to meet the Animal Master's eyes. "I have traveled far to speak with you."

The Animal Master looks down at the man. I know how this man must feel—suddenly small, suddenly weak. "What do you want of me, little man?"

The shaman draws back his shoulders and stands straighter, though I know he is cold and tired. He is strong, and I am glad to be one of his people. "My people need food," he says. "We eat berries and leaves and nuts, but they are not enough. We have watched the beasts hunt." His voice does not falter, though the Animal Master glares at him. "The animals—your beasts—could feed us, if you would let us hunt them."

The Animal Master's eyes are bright and hard. "Why should I let you hunt my beasts?"

The shaman does not flinch or step back. "We will be your people, just as the beasts are your beasts. We will care for the beasts that we take, and use their strength wisely. And we will always be your people. We are a strong people."

"You are strong?" says the Animal Master.

The shaman nods.

"Show me how strong you are," the Animal Master says, and where he stood, a dire-wolf stands.

The wolf bares his teeth and leaps at the shaman, but the man grabs him by the throat, locking his hands around the beast's neck. The wolf shakes himself and tosses his head, but the man holds steady.

The man lifts the wolf, hauling his front legs off the ground.

Then the wolf is gone. The man is clinging to a snake that twists in his grip. The snake wraps its body around the shaman's arm, but the man does not loosen his grip. The snake lashes out with its tail and I can see a streak of red on the man's chest where the tail has struck. But he does not let go.

The snake shifts, shimmering in the darkness. And the man clings to the neck of a deer—a buck—and he changes his grip to lock an arm around the neck of the beast. The buck tosses his head, but the beast is weakening, panting for breath. I can see the muscles in the shaman's arm trembling—though this is not a battle of muscle. This is a battle of spirit and the shaman is strong.

He grips the buck's neck tighter, so that the breath barely whistles in the buck's throat.

And so it is the Animal Master that the shaman holds by the throat. The Animal Master lies still in the shaman's grip, breathing quietly and watching the shaman with hard and bright eyes. The shaman releases him, and steps back.

The Animal Master lies still for a moment, then rolls to his feet. "Yes," he says. "You are strong."

The shaman does not move. "My people are strong," he says. "I came here for all my people."

Still the Animal Master studies him. "You could have choked me and taken my beasts," he says. "You did not."

The shaman's voice is harsh. "We need you. We need you to keep the animals well. We need you just as the beasts need you."

"You are wise, small man," says the Animal Master. "You will be my people and you will hunt my beasts. And when I need your help, your people will help me?"

"We will be your people," the shaman says again.

"It is well," says the Animal Master. "It is done." The dark wind blows around them and I cannot see the shaman. The man is gone and the Animal Master and the she-bear stand before me.

"You are one of his people," the Animal Master says. "When I ask for your help, you will come."

I shake my head in puzzlement. "You do not need my help. You are strong. I am young; I know little; I . . ."

"You are stronger than you know. You will learn. I will call you—not now. But when I call you, you must come."

"I will come."

He nods. "Now you have seen what you needed to see and you will go back to your world. I will . . ."

"Not yet," I say. My voice is steady. I look past the Animal Master to the great she-bear spirit. "First, there must be peace between me and the bear."

For the first time, the Animal Master's expression changes. He is amused. "Ah—already you try to use your strength. Do not overstep yourself, little shaman."

"I came to make peace," I say stubbornly. "There should be no battle between us." The bear glares at me. "The man who killed the beast did not understand our ways. He is . . ."

"He is your brother and you must account for him," the bear growls. She rears to her full height. "You are . . ."

"Stop this," the Animal Master says. The bear growls, but I cannot hear the words. She stops when the Animal Master glares at her. "What will you give for peace?" he asks me. "What can you give?"

I glare at him, looking into his amused eyes. "I have given all that I have," I say angrily. "I have given my tribe. I have no people and I am alone. I have nothing to give."

The she-bear growls and I can hear her words. "There will be peace," she says. "But only between me and this little man." She stares at me with sullen eyes.

126

She is a trickster spirit and I do not trust her. "Peace between you and I, and that is all."

I glare back at her. "Marshall is my brother. He must be safe from you."

"He is safe," she growls. "I do not want that one, that small and weak one."

I do not trust her. She nods her head and shows her teeth in a kind of grin. "Peace between us," she says and the silver sheen of her fur begins to fade. She is vanishing into the darkness. "Peace," she says, and she is gone.

I am left with the Animal Master. "Remember," he says. "I will come for you and you must help me then." He is fading, disappearing like mist in the sunlight. The world around me is growing darker.

"I will remember," I say. He is gone and I am alone in the darkness. Alone.

I beat the drum that I still hold in my hands. I beat a steady rhythm and the sound grows louder, a strong and powerful sound, like thunder over distant mountains.

The rain beats against my face. I open my eyes and the moon is a bright blur of light, barely visible through the clouds. The hard rock is cold against my back. My hands clutch the drum and the thunder rolls over the mountains.

We have a truce, the bear and I. I speak to the empty Valley. "There is peace," I say. "There is peace here." But the bear is a trickster spirit and I do not trust my own words.

The thunder rolls overhead like drumbeats and leaves only rain behind.

10

It is raining—just a hint of the winter weather to come. I am glad of the rain. It makes the Valley quiet. The birds make small, uncomfortable noises in the trees. New grass will grow and the deer will grow fat.

I sit in the opening of my hut, where I can look out at the Valley. For a moment, I have put aside my work—I have been stitching a pouch for the knuckle-bones of the bear. It will be a handsome pouch, made of the hide of a wild boar.

I am smoking the last of the tobacco that Marshall gave me. It has been almost a month since I left the Outside and returned to the Valley. I have become used to being alone again. I have not seen the bear spirit since I returned from my journey.

The rain is going away now and the sun is shining through the clouds. I step out of the hut. Sunlight glitters on the grass of the meadow, reflecting from raindrops.

"Hello, Sam!" Marshall's greeting echoes across the Valley. I see him, high on the rocky slope of the mountain. I lift a hand in greeting and he waves back.

He bounds down the slope, leaping from rock to rock. We meet at the foot of the mountain. He hugs me in greeting and I am glad he is here. We walk toward the flat rock and Marshall talks as we walk.

"I was planning to be here two weeks ago, but the

128

Court assigned me to be your guardian. You have no idea how much guarding you've needed. Between that and my dad's business ..." He pauses just for a moment when he mentions the business, then keeps talking. "I've been busy, that's sure." He talks so quickly, I had forgotten how quickly. "You're a star; a real celebrity. I've turned down invitations for talk shows, exclusive interviews, TV commercials ... I even had to go on a talk show myself, since you weren't available." He grins and, though I do not know quite why he is grinning, I grin back. "There's a director who wants to make a documentary about the Valley, but he's not the right one and there'll be others. There are reporters and promoters and ..." He shakes his head and shrugs. "I've been so busy guarding you, I didn't have time to come visit." He frowns and he seems much older. "You know, we should get that radio–telephone hookup I talked about, so ..."

"No," I say. "I do not want to talk to you through a machine."

He frowns again and, when he speaks, he speaks a little more slowly. "I just thought you could stay in touch better...."

"No," I say again. And I grin at him. "I will be here. You know where to find me."

I meet his eyes and he laughs suddenly, the laughter breaking through his frown. "It's good to be back, Sam. I'd forgotten ... I guess I'd better slow down for a minute and ..." He breaks off the sentence to laugh again. "I'll slow down."

He swings his pack off his shoulders beside the flat rock. "I brought tobacco," he says and that is the last thing he says for a time. We smoke together. He blows smoke rings and I watch them break apart in the breeze. When he does speak, it is to ask about my time in the Valley. "How's it been going?" he asks.

I look across the meadow, still glittering in the sunlight. I do not know how to tell him of the mixture of loneliness and happiness that I have felt. "It is a good Valley, a rich Valley," I say. "If my tribe were here. . . ." I stop and I shrug. "But it is a good place." He is watching my face.

"The bear and I are at peace now," I say. Again, I do not know how to speak to him of the journey that I made to meet the Animal Master. I know that he will not understand the ways of power. "I have made the tools of a shaman," I say. "I will show you. Later."

He nods, and I know that he is thinking of things that he must tell me. His shoulders are tight and his fist is clenched in his lap.

"You have other things to tell me," I say. "Say them and then you can relax and smoke with me."

He flattens the hand that was a fist. "That woman who met us at the Morgan Foundation," he begins. "The pale woman named Cynthia . . . she killed herself not long after she talked to us." He is looking down at his hands as if they are very important. "Morgan called and told me. He wanted to know what Cynthia had said to us. I told him as much as I could remember."

I remember the look on Cynthia's face when she ran back to the building. I am not surprised she is dead. I cannot be sad for her. She was afraid to be alive.

"I told Morgan what you had said about Moses and the spirits," Marshall is saying. "I didn't understand all of it, myself." He looks up from his hands for a moment. "Morgan seemed to understand."

"He needs to understand," I say. "He needs to know the spirits to understand himself."

Marshall studies his hands again. "I'd like to believe in all these spirits and things. I think I'd like the world more. But I can't."

I lay a hand on his shoulder. "You are all right as you are," I say. "You are fine."

He nods, but his shoulders are still tense. He leans back on his hands and gazes up at the mountains.

"You have more to say," I tell him.

He speaks quietly, as though he did not want to speak at all. "I'm going away for a while. I have to go to the Belt and take care of my dad's . . . of my business." He frowns and chews on his lower lip, then turns to look at my face. "I wasn't going to tell you until later. It doesn't seem right to come and then say that I'm leaving first thing. But I have to go. I'll be gone for three months or so. While I'm gone, James Andrews will take care of anything you need. But I feel bad about leaving. I just . . ." He spreads his hands before him, helplessly. "That's why I thought, maybe the telephone hookup . . ."

"I don't need anything from James Andrews," I say. Marshall is still frowning, not happy.

"I lived here before you came here," I say to him. "I lived alone with the beasts. I will not mind that."

"Andrews will check in on you anyway. Somebody should." He is shaking his head. "If you wanted, you could come with me. . . ."

I shake my head at him. "I have come to one new world. I do not want to leave it yet." I grin at him then. "And now you have said all the bad things that you needed to say. Can you stop frowning?"

He throws back his head and laughs. "All right, all right. I'll stop."

We sit and smoke and say very little again, and that is better. It is good to have him here. In the evening, we sit around the campfire to watch the moon rise. He tells me of plans that he has for the business and I listen to the sound of his voice, though the words make little sense. Prospectors and scout craft and stationary rigs and so many other words that I do not understand.

We hunt together. Marshall has brought a rifle for me and, to make him happy, I practice shooting. It is not as bad now as I thought before. A hunter could use a weapon like this—if he were careful to speak to

131

the spirit of the beast he killed and careful to pay his respects to the Animal Master.

I do not tell Marshall of the Animal Master. I know that he will not understand. I show him my drum and my pouch and the look on his face is probably the same look I wear when he talks of business.

On the last night that he is to be in the Valley, we are both quiet and Marshall frowns. "You will be back soon," I say. "We will hunt in the winter snows."

He nods. "I just wish I could stay. And I wish that I knew how the work in the Belt will go." He stops, staring out at the night. "I'm not my dad and I know it. But I want this to go well. I want to do as well as he would have."

The moon is full. It is rising over the Valley. When I move, the bones of the bear rattle in the pouch at my side. "A shaman can tell if a hunt will succeed," I say slowly. I take the bones from my pouch and hold them in my open hand. "I can throw the bones and tell you something—maybe good, maybe bad."

"You can tell? How?"

I show him the bones in the flickering firelight. "Each bone is marked—good side and bad. I throw the bones and the white sides show—it will be good. If the black sides show, it will be bad. If some are good and some are bad . . ." I shrug. "That is how the shaman of my tribe told the way of what was to come."

"You figure they tell what will happen?" he says.

"What may happen. The will of a strong man may change the will of the spirits," I say.

He takes a bone from my open hand and studies it.

There is a movement in the shadows beyond the circle of firelight. I can see the bear spirit watching from the darkness. Waiting. Marshall wears the claws around his neck and he is safe.

Marshall rubs the smooth bone and the bear steps closer. She does not speak, but Marshall glances up to speak to me. He frowns and follows my eyes, but sees nothing. Maybe he thinks I am watching the shadows; maybe he knows that I see something he does not.

The wind blows and he shivers suddenly. "No," he says then. "I don't think I do want to know what'll happen." He holds out the bone and I take it back. "The odds aren't good enough," he says. "I'll take my chances with ignorance."

The wind blows and the bear is gone, blown away like smoke on the wind. I slip the bones back into their pouch. Marshall does not believe in the ways of power. But sometimes, even without believing, he is wise.

The moon is high overhead. Marshall leans back to look at the pale circle. "I don't want to know if it won't work," he says softly. "My dad was building a new dream. That's good enough for me."

I remember sitting with Ben and listening to him speak of his dream. But Ben is gone, and the dream has lingered behind him.

We go to sleep when the moon is overhead. At dawn, I walk with Marshall to the top of the mountain slope. I watch him walk through the Barrier and away.

The Valley is quieter without him.

3

World in a Frame

11

My brother, Marshall, comes to the Valley on an afternoon touched with fog, greets me with a hug and a shout that makes the mountains rattle, and says that I must come with him to a film that is showing that night.

I have never been to a film—a moving picture, he calls it when I ask what it is—and I do not know why I should go to a film now. Eight winters have passed since my return to the Valley, and I have not gone Outside in all that time. I do not want to go Outside now.

But Marshall asks and so I go. I hike with him to the Barrier, carrying the clothes that I wore to the Trial and the key that lets me pass through the Barrier. I dress in the clothes—they smell a little of smoke, and the cuffs of the pants are marked with dirt, but Marshall says that he has other clothes for me at his house.

And we step into the world of the Outside. We hike to where Marshall's car waits by the strip they call a road.

The world moves faster here than in the Valley. The car speeds along the road—past square-cornered buildings and many other cars and people. At first a few people, then many people. Too many people. And Marshall's voice—always a little too loud in the Valley—is just loud enough to carry over the rumble of the engine and the sounds that are everywhere.

"This is the premiere. . . ." he begins.

"What is a premiere?" I interrupt.

"The first-time showing of this movie," he says.

I think about asking what a movie is, but decide that I will see. I wonder if we will see both the film and the movie.

"I want you to meet the lady who directed this," he says. "She's an amazing lady. And she wants to meet you."

I sit quietly, wondering how a lady directs a movie. To direct is to steer, just as Marshall steers the car. But I do not want to shout to ask. I will see.

Marshall turns the car from the road onto a smaller road that winds through trees. Unfamiliar kinds of trees, but still I am glad to see them. He stops by a building that stands alone in a green meadow.

"This is my house," he says, and grins. "Business is good." I nod. I never understand this business that Marshall talks of. I usually nod so that he will not try to explain it to me.

Inside the house, the rooms are too warm and I can smell the lingering odors of many people: cigarettes, pipes and sweet perfumes.

It is quieter here, though. Quieter than in the car or in the Outside, where the air seems to hum with sounds.

"What do you think?" Marshall asks.

I study his face. He has new wrinkles around his eyes since the last time that I saw him. But he is smiling.

"I think that we should sit and rest for a moment," I say.

Marshall nods, still smiling. "I think I've been rushing you."

I nod. "I think that you are right."

I have brought my pipe, of course. I sit on the floor where the carpet is much softer than the grass of the meadow. Marshall sits on a chair. I pack the pipe full

137

of tobacco and give it to Marshall to light. For a time, we smoke the pipe in silence, passing it back and forth as we always do. I think of many questions to ask but, for a time, I do not ask them.

Then I say, "How does this lady steer this movie?" Marshall looks puzzled and I say, "How does she direct it?"

He scratches his head. "I guess a director tells people what to do, for the most part."

"She steers people, then."

"I suppose you could say that. Then the people make the movie. I suppose. But you'd better ask her."

I wait while Marshall puffs on the pipe and blows a smoke ring. I have never learned to blow rings and I watch him with respect.

"This lady wants to make a film about the Valley?" I ask.

The last ring is lopsided, and Marshall blows the last of the smoke out in a puff. "How the hell did you figure that out? An hour ago, you didn't know what a film was."

I shrug. "Just after the Trial, you said that a director wanted to make a film about the Valley, but he was not the right one. Not a good person. I remembered that."

Marshall shakes his head in wonder. "Forgot all about that. How did you happen to remember? . . ."

"I do not know what may be important, so I try to remember as much as I can. That—I remembered," I say. "So is this lady director the right person?"

"You'll meet her tonight," he says. "You can judge for yourself. She's persuasive, that's for sure. She talked me into dragging you to this premiere. And she's persistent—fought her way through three layers of secretaries to talk to me. But you'll have to judge for yourself."

We smoke another pipe, then Marshall shows me how to work his shower. I wash, using the soap that

138

Marshall has for me. The soap has a smell of flowers that makes me sneeze when first I smell it—but I wash because Marshall has asked me to wash.

The clothes are dark blue pants and a shirt made of soft material. I rub the soft shirt-sleeve against my face to feel it. "I like this," I say.

Marshall grins. "I knew there was no way to get you into a suit. Clean jeans and a flannel shirt will have to do." He wears stiff-looking clothes and I am glad that I do not have to. "Let's go," he says.

And we go back into the Outside where everything moves faster. Into the car and past lights and people and buildings. The sky is crossed by lights that have no place there. Or would have no place in the sky of the Valley. Bright white lines of light that move across the sky and back.

"Spotlights," Marshall says. "That's where we're going." And we go.

A premiere is many people in a room filled with too many chairs. Or maybe that is a movie. I follow Marshall and he keeps a hand always on my shoulder. He tells me people's names and I nod and sometimes say hello. Marshall talks to the people and I try to smile.

"Sam." The voice beside me is soft. The woman who stands at my elbow is about my height. Her dark hair is cropped close to her head and she wears a silver headband. Her eyes are dark and quick like the eyes of a fox and she is smiling. "I wanted to ask you about hunting the deer, the . . ." and she uses the true name for deer, their name in the language of my people.

She uses the language of my people. I reach out to touch the shoulder of this small woman, who does not look at all like a woman of my people. "How did you know that word?" I ask. "Where did you learn it?"

She studies my face. "You talked about them at the Trial. I've watched the tape record a few times. Did I say the word right?"

"You said it right."

The lights overhead flash, and for a moment the chatter of many voices fades. The woman takes my hand from her shoulder and holds it for a moment. "I will see you later, Sam. Enjoy the movie."

Marshall turns back in time to see her moving away, and calls, "Merle!" She waves from the crowd.

"Talk to you after. . . ." and she is gone.

"That's Merle," he says to me. "The lady director I wanted you to meet."

I nod. If this lady steers people to make a film, she must do it well. I am glad that I came to this movie, this premiere, this film.

The lights dim and a curtain that covered the wall across from us lifts. Lights dance on the white wall and I see pictures in them—as I did on the screen that Amanda—*dark* showed me so long ago.

Pictures—an empty street. An animal—a rat—crosses the street, stops in the center to sniff at something that I cannot see, and runs on into the shadows. There is music in the room and I do not know where it comes from. But through the music, I hear a sound in the shadows. A young man—dressed in tight blue pants, like the ones I wear, and a black shirt—steps from the shadows. His eyes are the eyes of a hunter. He walks like a man stalking a deer—or being stalked by a hungry beast.

He turns toward a sound in the shadows and another young man steps from the darkness. Another young hunter, eyes bright and wary. "You ready?"

"Ready."

And suddenly, both have blades in their hands, blades that catch the light and glitter. The light glitters on the eyes of the men as they circle each other. Circling—each light on his feet. One man's blade flashes in; the other man moves to one side and counters. But misses.

They circle. Attack. Retreat. The larger man—the one who waited in the shadows—gets past the other man's defense to slash at his arm. Blood spreads—a dark stain on the black shirt.

They circle. I can hear their breathing. The smaller man is tiring—his blade is slower; he falters once, then again. The other man is not tired. He moves quickly. And at a moment when the tired man falters, the blade flashes out and catches the tired man's hand. The tired man's knife flips away to spin through the air.

I cannot see the fighters. The square of light on the wall shows only the knife that spins on the dark street, catching the light each time it turns. I hear a grunt, a small cry, then only one person breathes in the darkness. I hear footsteps running away; light, dancing feet.

The spinning blade slows and stops. Words that I cannot read roll past on the screen. I look into the faces of the people in the crowd, looking for the lady director, Merle. I cannot see her.

"It was a good fight," says the voice of a young woman. Her voice is husky and low, a little tired. "A clean fight, you know? Sure, someone died. You live in the street, sometimes you die in the street. It's like that. But it was a good fight."

The blade is gone and the young woman looks down at us from the wall. Her face is tired; her eyes are sad, even when she smiles. She talks for a while about her friends, people who live with her in the street. The pictures show fights—and sometimes cars with turning lights come to send the fighters running. The women are painted like Zee was painted—bright red lips and eyes circled with blue or green. They are dressed like Zee was dressed when I saw her at the Trial. I watch for Zee, but I do not see her.

I do not understand all that happens in the pictures or all that the voice of the young woman says. But then we are back—an empty street at night. Two people—a man and a woman. I recognize the woman with the tired eyes and tired voice. They circle. But this fight is not neat—she slashes the man once, then again. The dark street is marked with drops and patches of fallen blood. The man slips—and this time the pictures show him die.

And words that I cannot read roll over the picture that I did not understand.

The lights come on and the people are standing and clapping. Marshall is clapping too. They clap for a long time.

Then we push through the crowd. I follow Marshall, looking for the lady director, Merle. I want to talk to her.

We find her in the middle of a crowd of people who carry cameras and notepads. ". . . get that beginning shot?" one man is asking.

"A remote rig," she is saying. "We got some of our best footage that way."

"It isn't true that your connections among these people who live in the streets helped you to . . ." the same man begins.

"Turn my history to an advantage?" she says, grinning. "Nope, I came at this as an outsider. I don't belong in that world anymore. I'm respectable now." And she laughs, giving her words a different meaning. Yes, she would direct people well.

She sees me and Marshall through the crowd and calls to us. "Marshall. Sam. I want to talk to you, but I'm afraid they've got me surrounded."

"And you love it," Marshall calls back. She laughs.

A man with a microphone has crowded close to me and asks, "What did you think of the film, Sam?"

I choose my words carefully. "I wanted to see what was happening outside the box. This . . ." I hold up my fingers to form a square. ". . . was not enough."

The lady director is grinning. "He's right. A film is a window that sets a frame around the world. I change the world by putting it in a box. And the kind of world you get depends on what in the world you frame. I change the world by putting it in a different box." She laughs. "There—I managed to get some philosophy in there, despite you all. Now you can go back to your questions about my sordid past."

A woman starts another question, but the lady director holds up her hand and shouts over the people to Marshall and I. "Can I come to the Valley and talk to you?"

I nod and she waves her hand in a kind of salute. The woman in the crowd begins her question again and the others grin and write furiously.

"She plays well to a crowd," Marshall says as he drives me back to the Valley.

"She directs people well," I say, and he looks at me as if he is puzzled.

Marshall brings her to the Valley on a golden day when the sun is shining and the insects call in the meadow. A good day—the sun is warm on my bare back and legs. I am sitting at the flat rock near the hut and I am chipping a new knife, using a glassy black rock that I have found. This rock chips to a very sharp edge. The new knife will be sharper than my old flint knife.

I see them across the meadow—Marshall and a smaller person who takes two steps for each step of Marshall's. I lay down my tools and run to meet them.

When I hug Marshall in greeting, the bear claws around my neck rattle against the claws around his. I hesitate, not knowing how to greet the lady director. But she takes both my hands in hers and says, "Hello, Sam. The newspapers had a field day with your comment on my film."

"Is that good or bad?" I ask.

She grins. "In this case, good. We needed the publicity." She holds my hands in hers and I see that one of her arms is marked with a scar. She sees that I am

143

looking at the scar and turns her arm so that I can see the length of it. The thin white line curves from the bend of her elbow to the back of her hand. "An old scar," she says. "From a knife fight a long time ago."

I hold her hand and trace the scar with one finger. "You dropped your knife when you got this?" I say.

"I used my other hand," she says. "I could use it just as well." She is not smiling now.

"You won," I say.

"I was younger then," she says, and does not smile. "I won." Her eyes are the eyes of a hunter.

"You were hunting the wrong beasts," I say.

She nods. "I was young," she says again. "I'd like to hunt the right way."

I release her hand. "Maybe you will be able to learn."

Marshall stands beside us, frowning a little. "We can take her hunting, Sam. Late this fall or maybe in early spring."

I nod. Marshall does not hunt the right way. He is my blood brother, but still he does not know how to hunt. "She will hunt," I say.

We walk to the flat rock and I watch the lady director. She moves with the quick grace of a hunter. Her feet make little noise in the grass. Yes, she could learn to hunt as a person should hunt.

We sit on the flat rock and smoke together. She admires the knife that I have made and I say that it is hers—I like this woman. When she asks, I tell her how I hunt the deer. Her eyes are bright and alive and she listens to me as I listen to the sounds of the world when I am hunting.

She asks questions. How do you choose a deer to hunt? How do you stalk her? How do you strike?

I tell her of the hunt—of the sharp focus of the world when everything is bright and clear, when the scents are stronger and I feel the vibrations of the earth with my feet. I tell her of the end of the hunt—when the hunter takes the spirit of the beast and is one with the hunted.

She nods and leans back and I realize that she has been bent forward, as if to listen better. "That part where you see everything clearer sounds like filming," she says. "When suddenly you don't think, and you don't plan. You just do." She looks at Marshall. "You know what I mean?"

Marshall shakes his head. "I never understood Sam's way of hunting and I'll probably never figure out what you mean about filming."

He takes in a puff of smoke before passing the pipe to Merle. He blows a lazy smoke ring that drifts and starts to blow away. But the smoke changes, becoming grayer, darker. And where the smoke was, the bear spirit stands, watching Marshall with sullen eyes. She lifts her heavy head and asks me in the Old Tongue why these people are here. What are they doing in the Valley?

Merle had been talking softly to Marshall, joking about filming and hunting and things that I do not understand. But she stops and I know that she is watching me. "What's wrong, Sam?" she asks.

"The spirit of the bear is here," I say, and point toward the waiting spirit.

Merle looks, but does not see. She frowns and shakes her head. "Can't see what you're talking about."

Marshall blows the last in a series of smoke rings, glances in the direction of the bear, and shakes his head. "I've been looking for years, Merle, and I still can't see her. But she's the reason that I always wear these." He touches the bear claws around his neck.

The spirit growls at me and asks again in the Old Tongue why these people are in the Valley. I meet her angry eyes and ask her what concern that is of hers. She rears back on her hind legs and glares down at me.

"What are you saying?" Merle asks. "What does she want?"

"She wants to know why you are here," I say.

"Tell her that I am here to learn about this Valley—and maybe to make a film, if you'll let me."

I shake my head. "I cannot tell her about a film—there are no words."

"Just tell her I want to learn."

The bear is watching Merle. I tell the spirit what the lady has said. And the bear throws back her head and laughs—huh, huh, huh—a bear's grunting laughter.

I tell Merle that the spirit laughs and the lady frowns. "What's so goddamn funny?"

The bear says in the Old Tongue that these people cannot learn. They cannot hunt; they cannot learn to hunt; they do not see; they do not understand the world and they cannot learn.

I tell Merle and she shakes her head angrily. She glares at the place where the spirit stands laughing. "Seems like this spirit is pretty convinced of . . ."

"I can't believe you are taking this seriously," Marshall interrupts.

Her hands are fists in her lap. She unclenches them deliberately. "I don't much like dealing with a challenger that I can't even see," she says.

He shrugs. "If you can't see her, then you act like she isn't there."

"Yeah?" She looks at him steadily then reaches out and touches the claws that hang around his neck. "Then why do you wear these?"

He shrugs and looks uncomfortable. "I don't have to, I suppose." He holds the claws lightly in his hand. "I could take them off."

"No," I say. The bear has stopped laughing to watch Marshall's hand on the claws. "He must wear them," I say to Merle. "He does not see her and he does not believe, but I told him that he must wear them. They protect him, because he cannot protect himself."

Merle nods, still frowning. She looks back to the place where the bear sits. "She still here?" I nod. "Tell her that I will learn if you will teach me. Tell her to wait and see."

I tell her and she snorts and shakes her head. She says that no good will come of this. No good at all. And she fades into a mist that blows like a smoke ring across the grass.

"She's gone," I say.

"You'll teach me?" she asks.

I look at Marshall, who frowns and shakes his head. Then I look back to this strange lady with eyes like a hunter. "I'll teach you."

This evening, I roast a rabbit that I caught in a snare by the stream. We drink wine that Marshall carried in his pack. Marshall tells us about the stars that shine above the Valley. The storyteller of my tribe told stories about the stars—but those were different stars and different stories. Marshall tells us that each star is like the sun. He tells us that some have other worlds with them. I do not understand all that he says, but I nod. He tells us their names and how far they are. Merle leans back in the half-circle of his arm and Marshall smiles.

It is good to have them here. Marshall is glad and I am glad. I like this strange woman who is so different from women of my tribe.

They sleep in a small tent that Marshall has set up by the hut. I sleep where I always do, under the ledge of the rock outcropping.

I can hear the gentle murmur of their voices in the tent and the rhythm of their breathing, first slow, then quicker and louder when they make love. I hear small cries of gladness from Merle. And then the soft sound of their breathing as they sleep.

I am glad that they are here. The bear is wrong, I know.

I awaken at dawn, curled comfortably in the grass under the overhang. When I stand, birds fly in alarm from the rock. The meadow is wakeful with the small sounds of birds and animals. I take my spear and my knife and I walk away from the camp into the meadow.

At the spring, I splash water over my head and shake myself dry. I choose a few small stones from beside the spring.

A tiny sound—like the scratching of a bird in the grass—makes me look up. " 'Morning, Sam," says Merle. Her voice is very soft, pitched to match the sounds of the morning around us. She steps past me to the spring and splashes water on her face. Her movements are small and precise—like those of a fox. Neat and careful. "I can never sleep late," she says. "There are always too many possibilities in the air. Too much in the wind."

I am not sure I understand her. But I say, "Many things in the wind. Can you smell the rain that's coming?"

She grins. "Rain and thunderheads and potential calamity—they're always in the wind. Film-making is a rough business." She takes a deep breath and looks at me; I frown. "Sorry, Sam. I talk nonsense in the morning. Were you on your way somewhere? I didn't mean to stop you."

I open my hand to show the stones I hold. "To hunt a rabbit. If you will be silent, you can come."

She nods, grinning. "I'll shut up."

Her sandals are silent in the grass, unlike Marshall's boots. I follow the small breeze that blows down the Valley, letting it tickle my face and bring me the scent of the day. I stay near the stream where the bushes are thick.

Not far away, a buck rabbit grazes near the cover of a bush. I stop and Merle stops just behind me—still silent. With a sudden flick of my arm, I lob one small stone at the rabbit and catch him as he leaps forward. He falls, stunned.

I run to him before he can recover and slit his

148

throat with the stone blade that I carry at my belt. Silently, the beast's small spirit joins mine. There is strength, even in a rabbit.

Merle is at my side, watching. "Why the stone knife?" she asks. "Why not steel?" She points to the sheath knife at my side.

"There is a power in the stone that the steel lacks," I say. "Stone is for bloodletting and freeing the spirit." I hang the rabbit at my belt. "Now we can talk," I say.

She is silent for a moment more, as we walk beside the stream. I am glad of that. I am glad she knows how to be silent.

"I want to make a film about this place and about you," she says softly. "I need to understand how you live."

I nod. "I have said I will teach you. What else do you need to make this film?"

"Money," she says, "but it shouldn't be hard to find backing after this last film." Then she puts her hands in her pockets and stares at the granite mountains. "People. The right people." And I can see her thinking about the right people. "In the end, it's the people who matter. We have to work together—solid people. Really solid."

"Like the tribe," I say.

She lets the silence stay for a moment, then puts her hand on my shoulder. "You know, sometimes I forget how it must be for you. You're so far from your people."

I say, "I do not understand how it is for your people. Marshall has a family—but he does not seem to care for them or them for him. They do not seem to . . ." I link the fingers of my two hands and form a unit of them.

Merle nods. "I never had a family—not really. Left my mom when I was eleven. We live differently than you, Sam. We choose our own company, our own family, our own tribe. We find the right people." She looks at my face. "Maybe you can find a new tribe here."

I think then that she can learn—learn quickly and learn well. We walk in silence back to the camp. Marshall meets us at the flat rock. Sleep is still in his eyes. Merle grins at him. "We are going to make a film, Sam and I."

"Oh, yeah," he says sleepily. "When?"

"In the spring," she says, then looks at me. "The weather is good in the spring?"

"Clear days with a little frost. Green grass. Snow by the stream. The spring is good."

"By spring, I'll have a backer and a crew and a story line," she says. She stretches her arms toward the sun and almost dances forward, tumbles feet over hands in the grass and lands on her feet—like the birds that tumble in flight for no reason but joy. "By spring."

By spring, she will understand more of the world and how it works. By spring, she will be a hunter. Perhaps I can begin a new tribe here in this new world. By spring.

Marshall returns to the Valley alone. We smoke a pipe together and I know that he is nervous. He does not blow smoke rings. "What do you think of Merle?" he asks abruptly.

"She can learn," I say. "She can learn the ways of the hunter."

"Do you like her?" he asks.

I nod. Yes, I like her. I do not trust her—she has the eyes of a hunter who does not know how to hunt.

Marshall is studying my face. "I am going away on business for a while, Sam. Probably for most of the winter."

"Where will you go?" I ask. I puff the pipe calmly. I do not want my blood brother to know that I will worry while he is gone from here.

He looks up at the sky, where a sliver of moon shines in the twilight. "Up to the moon. We're having problems with our mining operations there. I'm not sure how long I'll be needed there."

Out of even this strange world where I now live. I nod, and try to keep my face calm. Ben died on the moon.

"I'll be back," he says. "By spring most likely. And Merle will come to visit often."

He says that he will be back, but when I hug him in farewell, I think that he may be gone forever. And in the nights that follow, I watch the white face of the moon with sorrow and anger.

Merle comes to the Valley to learn. She comes alone, hiking down from the ridge with wine and tobacco in her pack. Each time, she stays for a few days—maybe three, maybe five.

I teach her: I show her how to skin a rabbit; how to set a snare; how to catch the fire with bow and tinder; how to choose the wood for a spear shaft; how to scrape it smooth and season it; how to chip a spearhead from flint and bind it to the shaft with the sinew of a deer. I make her a sheath for her stone knife. She learns the ways of the toolmaker and her hands are quicker and more clever than before.

"You must learn the ways of the beast," I say to her, then. I teach her to sit still—like the fawn in the grass. I teach her to watch and learn. In the morning, I leave her on the slope of the mountain; in the afternoon, I come back and ask what she has seen.

"A herd of deer passed this way," she says.

"How many?" I ask. "How many were bucks, how many does? What did you learn by watching them?"

She learns to read the signs that she did not see before. She learns. Late in the evening, we sit by the fire and we talk. "Marshall could not learn to sit still in the grass," I say to her. "He could not learn to wait."

She nods. "I can be patient—when I want something."

"What do you want?"

"I want this film to work. I want to show what it is like here," she says. She stares into the fire. Outside the circle of firelight, the beasts roam the night. "There are no animals left on the Outside. Or just about none. Once there were whales and wolves and buffalo and beasts. Now there are human wolves who hunt each other."

"Where did the beasts go?" I ask. "Did you hunt them too much?"

"No. We changed their world around them. Took away the trees where the hawks and eagles nested and where the deer ran to hide. Laid roads over mountains and pipelines over cold, frozen lands. Changed rivers and closed off lagoons. We changed the world and the animals could not change to match."

"The Animal Master took them back," I say softly. And I tell her of the Animal Master, the one who made all the animals so long ago. Before the Animal Master let the animals into the world, the people lived on nuts and fruits that they gathered. A powerful shaman traveled to find the Animal Master—because the tribe needed better food to make their spirits strong. And the Animal Master said that the animals could be hunted—but only as long as the people treated the animals with respect. If the people did not hunt well and did not take care of each animal's spirit, the Animal Master would take the beasts away.

"He took them away," Merle says. She is silent and in the Valley the beasts walk.

She learns. At the stream when we stop to drink, I ask, "Who has passed this way?"

She squats to study the ground. She is silent for a moment, breathing quietly as a hunter must breathe. She lightly touches the ground where a hoof has scraped against it. She stands and pads on bare feet to the side of the water. On a bush, she finds a tuft of coarse hair;

she finds prints in the softer ground by the stream. "Wild horse," she says, then, ". . . followed by a wolf. A lone wolf. A big one—probably a male." She looks at me and I nod. Then I show her how the print of the horse shows that the beast stood for a while to drink and did not run when he left. The wolf's prints are old—he did not follow the horse; he went before.

Merle listens and she learns.

On a sunny day, she leaves the Valley, saying that she will not be back for two weeks. I walk with her to the Barrier.

She is alert; she catches the scent of the wild horse on the wind, notices where a wolf has rested, leaving a small hollow in the grass. And not far from the Barrier, she finds a place where the sand is marked with the scraping of claws. "I don't know what passed by here," she says. "I haven't seen these prints before."

"Cave bear," I say. Her paw-prints are broad and deep, but still she is a young bear. I show Merle a red-brown hair, caught on a blade of grass. I point out the path that the bear followed. And after Merle goes to the Barrier and back to the Outside, I follow the bear.

I follow the scent that lingers; I find the marks of her claws—and I know where she is going. I go alone up the mountain to the cave of the bear.

I know this place, though I do not often come here. I recognize the tumble of rocks where the bear fell when Marshall shot her.

Beasts and rushing waters from melting snows have scattered her bones. I see the skull, wedged between two rocks where the winter rains must have carried it. The dark eye sockets watch me. I can smell the young she-bear strongly now; she must live here, in the old she-bear's cave.

"Are you here?" I ask in the Old Tongue. The bear that comes from the darkness of the cave is the old she-bear spirit; her claws make no sound when they scrape against the rock. She stops at the mouth of the cave and comes no further.

"The woman is learning," I say to her in the Old Tongue. "She is learning the ways of the hunt and the ways of the tribe."

The spirit shakes her head and says in the Old Tongue that the woman will not learn the ways of the tribe; she is an Outsider and will always be an Outsider. She cannot learn.

"She will be one of the tribe," I say. "A new tribe in this world."

The spirit laughs at me. She does not speak; she only shakes her head and laughs. I hear the scrape of claws against rock and the young she-bear stands in the mouth of the cave.

The spirit fades; the young she-bear growls a warning, snapping her jaws and tossing her head at me. I back away from the cave, heading down the mountain. Laughter and growls follow me down.

I am alone in the Valley. Winter is coming and the days grow colder. I have grown used to Merle's company and I am lonely.

One morning, I awaken to the smell of snow on the wind. The sun is dim and far away and I am cold—colder than I should be on a day when the sun is shining. Cold and alone.

I walk into the meadow and I see the herd of deer grazing on the far side of the Valley. The spirit of the old buck who is a part of me belonged to this herd. The spirit rises in me and I feel the need to be a part of the herd. I want to be with them.

My spear, I leave by the flat rock; my knife, I leave beside the spear. I walk toward the herd—my head up like a buck, my footsteps silent in the grass. Though the deer look up to see me, they do not run. I am one of them—cloaked in the spirit of the old buck.

I walk among them and they return to grazing. I

can smell the warm breath of them in the cool air. I feel the weight of my antlers on my head; I can smell the sweet scent of the grass. A fawn looks up from where she grazes at her mother's side. A late-born one—still small for this time of year. She steps toward me, curious. She does not recognize this old buck.

I gently touch her neck and she tosses her head but does not move away. I stay near this fawn and her mother as we wander with the herd across the meadow.

I scent a saber-toothed cat behind us, and I lift my head to watch her pass. She is not hunting now, but we move away, trotting slowly toward the far side of the meadow. I put myself between the cat and the fawn and I move with the herd.

There—on the breeze from the mountain, there is a new scent that makes me lift my head, as all in the herd lift their heads. A scent and a sound that is at once familiar and strange. "Hello, Sam." A high voice like the calling of a hawk. "Hello."

A young buck snorts and paws at the grass. Another tosses his head and trots a few steps. Then in an instant, the herd turns and runs—away, away, away to the far reaches of the meadow.

I do not run. I stand in the meadow and watch Merle come toward me. "Hello, Sam! We've got backing for sure now—a major network. And I've talked one of the best wildlife cameramen around into working on the film."

For a moment, the words do not make sense to me. I am an old buck, ready to run. And this woman has the eyes of a hunter. I do not trust her. Then she hugs me in greeting and I am myself. "It's all going to work, Sam," she says. "It's coming together."

She holds my hand as we walk back to the flat rock and I feel almost as I did when I was with the herd. I am part of something that is larger than myself. She talks about the crew and the story line and the equipment they will need.

"A couple of ground cars, I'd guess. And a 'copter run . . ." She is talking quickly and I remember watching her talk at the film premiere, talking quickly, thinking quickly, moving quickly.

I catch one of her hands as she gestures and I say, "No ground cars. They tear up the grass. I have seen them." She looks startled. "And the 'copter will scare the beasts—you should try not to use it."

She frowns. "One ground car then. We'll need . . ."

"You will destroy what you want to show," I say, and I keep my hold on her hand. "You are thinking like an Outsider, not like a hunter who belongs in this Valley." I feel the tension in the hand that I hold. "Think like a hunter."

She looks out over the Valley. And the tension in her hand eases and she shakes her head. "Sorry, Sam. I've been on the Outside too long. I want this to work and . . ." She shakes her head again. "One 'copter run to bring in the equipment. I'll work out a way to do without the ground cars. It'll take longer. But . . ." She shrugs. "I'll just explain that it'll take longer. I'll make it work."

I put my hand on her shoulder and I say, "I will help you make it work." And she smiles; she looks tired but she smiles.

This evening, I build a fire on the flat rock and we roast a rabbit that I snared by the spring. "I brought champagne to celebrate," she says, and I nod and wonder what champagne is.

Champagne is wine that has come alive with bubbles. Merle opens the bottle when we have eaten the rabbit and the pop of the cork silences the insects in the meadow for a moment.

She clicks her cup of champagne against mine, and says, "To success. Success of the film and success for us both." I drink the bubbling wine when Merle does and wonder at this small ceremony. Merle sets down her cup and shivers. "It's getting cold. Winter's here."

"It will be short this year," I say. "But tomorrow there will be snow. I can smell it in the air."

She nods. "Wish I could predict as well." She studies my face. "Marshall told me that you can predict the success of a hunt by throwing the bones. Will that work for a film?"

"Marshall does not believe in the bones," I say.

"Marshall does not believe in a lot of things."

"The bones may say that the film will fail," I say. "If that is so, will you go home and try another day?"

She laughs. "Ah, I can just see trying to explain to the network, 'We can't do it just now. The bones say that we'll fail.' No, we can't quit. But at least I'll know what I'm fighting and I'll keep that in mind."

I shake my head. "You are following a path. You say you cannot turn. Does it do any good to know the end?"

She lays a hand on mine. "It does if the end is good. I need to know."

She wants so much for the film to succeed. I take the bones from the pouch in the hut and I smooth the ground before her. I give her the three bones: each smooth on one side and marked with a blackened notch on the other. "I rubbed them smooth with sand and carved the notch," I say. "They have only the power that I have given them."

"That's power enough, I'm sure." She rolls them in her hand, studying them.

I chant softly in the Old Tongue, asking for a successful hunt. Merle casts the bones. Two fall in the light, smooth side up. The third bounces on the uneven ground and falls in the shadows at my feet. The notch is on its upper side.

Merle looks at the third bone—her face is turned from the fire. Half is in shadow; half is lit with the firelight. "What does that mean, Sam? Two good; one bad."

I shrug. "You will succeed, but not as you expect.

157

You will lose, though you succeed. Or ..." I shrug again.

"Ambiguous, eh?" She frowns. She looks tired, and I put my hand on her shoulder as I scoop the bones from the ground and put them away. "Well, I guess I know that there is some trouble ahead. Nothing new. I wonder what I should watch out for."

"Watch out for the bear," I say softly. "She will trick you. She will make trouble."

Merle nods. "Hard to watch for something you can't see."

The moon is rising. I light a pipe and we share it. Merle is teaching me to blow smoke rings. But the wind blows them away. She shivers in the wind. I put my arm around her shoulders and she leans against me. "I wish I were like Marshall and I didn't believe in things." I am sorry that I let her throw the bones. I remember my younger sister; I remember a time that she burned her hand in the fire and I comforted her. I do not understand why Merle hurts, but I stroke her hair to comfort her. "I don't want to sleep alone tonight," she says.

She curls up beside me, in the hollow where I sleep, and her sleeping bag is large enough to cover us both. I put my arms around her and hold her so that she will be warm. I remember the warmth of my tribe around me. I have not slept with such warmth since I left my tribe. I have been alone.

She is so small within the circle of my arms. She rests her head on my shoulder. I stroke her hair; her body is warm against mine and my hand moves to stroke her back and legs, as I would have touched a woman of my tribe, once I became a man. Now, I am a man and I have no tribe.

Her scent is changing—it is at once familiar and strange. I remember being a buck and walking beside the doe. I remember the scent of the doe in season.

Her hands are small and warm and she guides my

hands to stroke her breasts. I do not understand the customs of her people. But her hands guide me and I mount her as I would mount a woman of my tribe. I listen to her small moans in the darkness. She is so small, so smooth, so different—but she is part of my tribe now.

Her hands stroke me and I am warm, surrounded by this strange woman who is one of my people. At last, a long time later, we sleep.

12

The snow that lingers on the slopes of the ridge is old and crusted; no new snow has fallen for many days. Patches of white hide in hollows near the stream, but the grass in the meadow is green and the sun is warm.

This day, Merle will be coming—with a 'copter and a crew. One 'copter run, she said, to bring in the equipment.

I hear the 'copter before I see it—a distant roar that echoes from the mountains. I return to the hut from the bank of the stream, where tender new shoots are growing.

The monster is awkward in the air, awkward and noisy as it lands. The sound hurts my ears and I stand far away, in the shadow of the hut.

The blade on top is still whirling when the door opens. A man jumps down and runs toward me—a pale man who runs with a clumsy gait. But around his neck I see the bear claws.

"Sam!" My blood brother Marshall embraces me and I look into his tired eyes. His face is lined and thin. "It's great to be back." He grins at me. "I know, I know. I've got to hunt and spend time in the sun and gain back the weight I lost. The moon colony isn't what you'd call a garden spot." He looks across the Valley at the mountains. "I'm glad to be back."

The blade of the 'copter has stopped whirling, and there are people: people carrying boxes, strange machines, racks of lights, cases, metal tubes—all hard and shiny and out of place in my Valley. Merle is with them—she hugs me in greeting.

I sit on the flat rock with Marshall and I watch. I did not know how confusing, how much, how many people there would be. The deer on the far side of the Valley lift their heads to watch. I feel as I felt when I first left the Valley for the Outside and I think with longing of the quiet places high in the mountains.

Marshall keeps one hand on my shoulder and tells me of his time on the Moon. "There's a constant hum in the tunnels," he says. "Air pumps, water pumps, generators. It's so quiet here." It is not quiet.

I watch Merle and the people I do not know. Merle is quick, running, talking to the men who are carrying boxes, directing the arrangement of equipment by the hut, helping people who are setting up a shelter. She grins in my direction but she does not stop running.

At twilight, the 'copter leaves—with a roar that frightens the deer on the far side of the Valley. Of the strangers, four remain behind—three men and a woman. Merle stands near them, but a little apart from them. The sound of the 'copter fades. The silence comes back to the Valley.

They look lost, these strangers, now that the machine has flown away.

"Come and smoke with us," I call to them, and I

take my pipe from the pouch at my belt. Merle sits on one side of me; Marshall on the other. They seem too solemn, this circle of people. They all sit silently, their legs crossed beneath them, their hands still. When they were working earlier, they talked constantly, shouted, laughed. I do not know how to set them back in motion.

I pack the pipe and pass it to Merle. She takes a little smoke in, and blows a smoke ring. And another. A third—and the smoke and laughter burst from her. She looks around the circle. "Will you get off your goddamned good behavior? You're making me nervous."

And the silence is broken. "Hey, Merle," the woman begins. "We figured this was a sacred smoking ceremony like the peace pipe. . . ."

"You wouldn't know a peace pipe if . . ." the tallest man begins.

"Oh, yeah. Well, let me tell you about . . ."

And the clatter and confusion that seems natural to these people is back. Joking and laughter and the feeling that they are a family.

Merle grins at me. She introduces the strangers. "Tim, Chris, Keith, and Pam. Tim is our cameraman; Chris does everything Tim and Pam don't do. Pam is our audio technician. And Keith does my worrying for me."

Keith grins at me. "She exaggerates. We alternate shifts—when I'm worried, she's not. When she's worried . . ."

"But I never worry, Keith," Merle says, grinning. And she laughs. I had forgotten—she directs these people. When she laughs, I know that they are with her, part of her tribe. And she seems almost like a stranger to me.

This evening, we roast a haunch of deer over the open fire. Tim, a tall man with ruddy skin and strong arms, tends the fire. Pam chops vegetables into a salad. We pass a bottle of wine from hand to hand.

161

Merle and Marshall and I sit together on one side of the fire. "It'll be a good project," Merle says. She takes the pipe from Marshall, takes in a puff of smoke, and lets it trail slowly from her lips. "It's the people that matter. These are good people." She is relaxing and, once again, she fits here—in this Valley with Marshall and I.

"It's dinner," says Tim. He slices the meat with a sharp metal knife and each person takes a share.

I have a memory of my tribe. I sat on my mother's lap and chewed on a scrap of meat. Around me, the tribe talked in low tones, laughing, joking. I think that it was a feast day—I remember that the shaman chanted the old legends and the fire burned late. The memory is good.

Merle stands and lifts her glass of wine. The people—her people—look to her. She is a small woman but, with the firelight in her eyes, she seems larger. "A toast," she says. "To Sam, the provider of the feast."

"To Sam," they say together and drink their wine.

I do not understand these people. I do not know their customs. But I feel warm among them. The pipe—not my pipe but another—is passing from hand to hand and the smoke smells sweet, like the herbs the shaman smoked. I take from the pipe and the world is brighter and clearer. I am among friends here and I am happy.

Tim, the cameraman, sits beside me and plays a stringed box that he calls a guitar. He says that he will teach me how to play. He starts to teach me the words to a song that I do not understand called "Ain't Misbehavin'."

When Merle leaves the fire with Marshall, she touches my shoulder lightly. "I'll see you in the morning, Sam," she says. I understand when she touches my shoulder that she will go with Marshall this night. I do not understand their customs, but among my people, the woman chooses. I nod.

162

I sleep by the fire. I can hear the breathing of the people around me. I am glad that they are here.

I awaken just before dawn, when the birds in the meadow are starting to scratch in the grass and make small sounds. Tim snores a little not far from me.

I stand and the birds near me fly with a whir of wings. Tim blinks and sits up. " 'Morning," he mutters. "You going somewhere?"

We climb the granite slope of the mountain before the sun is fully up. Tim walks silently in the grass of the meadow and on the granite slope. "I'm half-Indian," he says when I tell him he walks like a hunter. "Half-Cheyenne on my mom's side. I spent my summers with my granddad before he died. I learned a few things."

Tim grins when the deer do not run from us, but only trot a few steps from our path. He shakes his head and grins when we startle a cave hyena in a gully on the slope. When we look down at the Valley from the slope of the mountain, he shakes his head and grins. "It's big, Sam. And the camera will only see this much of it." He holds up his hands a short distance apart. I nod. "I liked what you said about Merle's last film," he says. "It takes most people a long time to figure out how different that frame on the screen is from the world that we filmed. We shut a lot of things out."

We sit together on the slope of the mountain and Tim talks about what they want to film. He talks about point of view and how the world is different through the camera lens. He talks about Merle and Marshall and Chris and the others and how they all look at the world from different angles. "Now I come at things from all angles and there's only one of me. Sometimes, I see the world as an Indian; sometimes, a cameraman." He shrugs. "It's confusing."

I like this man named Tim. I know that he wanted

to climb the mountain with me and talk because he wants me to be his friend. He directs people, just as Merle directs people. But I like him. I am glad of his company when we climb down the mountain.

It is a good day, this first day. Merle and I lead the others around the Valley. "Orientation," Merle calls it.

Merle is alert now, relaxed. At a bend in the stream, she stops and looks at me. She gestures upwind and says, "Mammoth." And I nod.

We follow the edge of the clearing in which a bull mammoth browses. Merle grins at me and points out the tracks of a deer by the side of the stream—one of the small, shy deer that hide in the brush. She tells them about the animals in the Valley and the mountains, and where they live and how a hunter tracks them.

Marshall trails behind the others, and I see him frowning a little. We are on the slope of the ridge when he calls out to Merle, "You can't climb up that way."

But Merle has already scaled the rock, just as we have done many times before. I follow her, but Marshall leads the others around the side of the steep slope. "You shouldn't risk ..." he starts to say to Merle.

She stops him. "When there's snow, it's a risk," she says. "Just now ..." She shrugs. "It's no problem." She is quick and quiet and sure, and I know that I have taught her well.

We climb the shoulder of the mountain, eat lunch, then follow a gully down to the meadow. Merle leads the way down with Tim at her side. They are talking—talking quickly like the babble of the stream—about possibilities and angles and filters and ... many things that I do not understand. Pam, Chris, and Keith follow them.

I walk with Marshall, behind the rest. He is limping. His face is red from the sun. He is watching Merle far ahead. "I thought she was a city kid," he says.

"She has learned much this winter," I say. And I tell him about the winter—about teaching Merle to find the burrows of rabbits and to pick the nuts that cling to the trees. I tell him of climbing the slopes in the snow and showing her safe snow and bad snow. I tell him about the new caves we have found in the mountain. Many things. "She belongs here now," I say to him. He looks down at his hands—pale beneath the dirt and scratches. "Just as you belong here," I say. "You and Merle are both part of my tribe."

He does not smile. He puts his hands in his pockets and watches Merle gesture as she talks to Tim. "You have been sleeping together while I was gone," he says.

I nod. I understand that he does not mean sleeping; Merle has explained this to me.

Marshall is frowning. "Then how did you feel? . . ." He hesitates. "Last night, Merle went with me. And you slept alone. How do you feel? . . ." The words trail away.

I put a hand on his shoulder. His muscles are tense and he watches Merle. "You are my brother, Marshall. You are one of my tribe." I stop, trying to find the right words. "I was not alone. We are all together." Still he does not smile. "You are my blood brother, Marshall."

He shakes his head. "Blood brothers can share a woman?"

I do not understand him. Share? We could not share Merle, because we do not have Merle. Merle has Merle and she chooses who to sleep with, within the bounds of the tribe.

"You are not angry?" he asks.

This I can answer. "I am not angry. I am glad that you are here."

165

His shoulders relax. "I don't understand you any better than I understand her, Sam. But I believe you." He smiles at me.

Together, we follow the others down the mountain. "So she's learned her way around the Valley," Marshall says as we are walking. "Has she seen the bear spirit?"

"No," I say. I have not seen the bear for many days. I have never seen the bear when Merle is in the Valley.

Marshall grins at me. "Maybe she hasn't changed so much after all. Maybe not."

At the fire that evening, Merle says, "Tomorrow, we begin." And she talks to Tim about cameras and lighting. And I wonder where the bear spirit is wandering and whether that is her laughter I hear on the breeze.

I awaken to fog—a chill, wet mist covers the Valley and hides the mountains from view. Keith, the first to emerge from his tent, scowls at the day. "God damn," he mutters. "I thought it was supposed to stay clear in the spring." He walks out to stand beside me. He reminds me of the small men of the Court—the ones who talked of benefits and costs and such. He frowns as they frowned. "When do you think it'll clear?" he asks.

"A few days," I say. "Why do you frown?"

"When we lose time, we lose money," he says, and he turns back to the camp.

Tim frowns at the fog; Chris frowns when he sees Tim's face. Pam looks worried and Keith paces. Merle, when she crawls out of her tent, grumbles at them, not at the weather. "You guys think you're going to get out of work just 'cause we have one day of rotten weather? Ha!" She rubs both hands back over her short hair and stretches. "Tim, I want you to go with Sam—get him to show you the best spots for blinds. Pam, I want you to check over your equipment; it's

166

liable to have gotten screwed up in transit. Chris, check out the possibilities for lighting that flat rock; we may need to do some close-up work there." She yawns again and squints at the sky. "Just as well to have rotten weather now—we couldn't have filmed today, anyway."

At noon, the rain begins. Tim and I are far from the camp, beneath the trees. The sky is a sullen gray and the rain is a steady drizzle. "How long do you think it'll rain?" Tim asks.

"Maybe a few days," I say, and this time I do not ask why he frowns.

Marshall and Tim use ropes and a tarpaulin to rig a shelter beside the rock outcropping. We sit by a small fire under the shelter. Tim plays the guitar and we pass the wine. It is a good evening. Merle says that the next day will be better. Even when Pam says that she cannot get rid of the hum in the sound system, Keith does not swear too much.

In the morning, the wind begins—a steady blast that shakes the tents and drives rain beneath the shelter and through the open door of the hut.

Merle is the first one awake. She makes pancakes on the camp stove and hands plates to each person as they crawl from their tents and run through the rain to the shelter. "You want truth in cinema," she says to Keith. "We got it. If rain and rotten weather aren't truth, I don't know what is."

Pam huddles in the hut with her sound system. Tim sits beneath the shelter and mournfully plucks his guitar. Keith paces. Marshall tries to talk to Merle, as she sits beneath the shelter with her chin in her hand, but gives up when she will not reply. He sits with Chris and they play a game called chess. Chris has brought a chess set with him. I wander away, across the valley—but the deer are hiding and the air is cold and wet.

When I go back to camp, nothing has changed. Merle

sits beneath the shelter, huddled against the chill. I sit beside her. "It's got to get better, doesn't it?" she asks me softly.

"It has only been raining one day," I say.

"It's been raining forever," she says. And I remember how quickly the world moves on the Outside. "The light is bad. Pam can't find the mysterious hum. Tim says that he'll try shooting in this if it stays." She shakes her head. "It'd be better if we had some film in the can. This way . . ." She shrugs.

That evening, the camp stove will not burn steadily—the flame flares and flickers with each gust of wind. Tim plays only sad songs on his guitar. Keith—though he sits still—looks like he should be pacing.

"Hey," Merle says to Tim. "You want to know how long it took for us to get that opening shot for the last movie? We were hanging out in the street for weeks and wasting film and . . ."

Tim tells her about a film he shot in a place called Florida where an alligator—probably one of the last, he says—ate his camera and almost got his assistant. Chris grins.

Keith stops looking worried and tells about a location in Africa where they had to haul in water at a phenomenal cost.

And when they are done, they do not seem to think the rain is as bad. I do not understand them. I look at Marshall, Marshall looks at me and we shrug. But that evening, for a while, they are happy.

That night, a tent blows down and I awaken to the sound of flapping canvas and steady cursing. By the time that Keith has struggled from beneath the wet tent, Merle and Tim are awake and helping.

Tim says that Keith should take his tent—he will share my spot beneath the shelter. Keith goes back to bed and Tim and Merle and I stand beneath the flapping tarpaulin.

168

"Why such bad luck?" Merle mutters, staring out at the darkness. She looks at me. "The bones were two good, one bad—not all three bad."

I shrug. "That is true." On the wind, I think I hear the laughter of the bear. I look to the direction from where the wind blows, but I see nothing.

Merle is watching me. She is listening to the wind. "Something up, Sam?"

I shake my head. Tim pats her shoulder and says, "I'll see what I can do tomorrow despite the weather."

In the morning, Tim and I leave at dawn. When we leave, the rain is a drizzle. There are no deer in the meadow. I find the tracks of the mammoth, but no beast. The wild horses have fled. The bison are gone. We are caught in a downpour and we return in the afternoon—wet and hungry.

It is not a good evening. Merle is pacing. Back and forth, back and forth, with her hands buried in her pockets and droplets of rain glistening in her dark hair. Tim and the others have gone to bed; Marshall and I are waiting for her to tire. Marshall is frowning. I smoke my pipe and watch her pace.

"In the streets, I had to buy off a couple of gang leaders," she says. "So that accidents would stop happening to my equipment." She shakes her head. "How do you buy off the weather?"

She paces—back and forth, back and forth. "You've got to rest sometime, Merle," Marshall says at last. "This isn't doing you any good. It's a run of bad luck and you can't do anything about it."

"I can pace," she says and glares at him. And she paces like the wolf in Amanda—*dark*'s cage. "I've never had bad luck like this before."

Do I hear laughter?

Merle stops pacing to watch my face. "Do you know why my luck is so bad right now?" She watches my face and I do not speak. "You told me once to watch out for the bear." Still, I do not speak. "I should have

169

learned more about this spirit, Sam. Could it be that she's the heavy that I have to buy off? Could she be doing this?"

I nod reluctantly. "She could."

"Is she?"

I shrug uncomfortably. "She has not talked to me for . . ."

"Can you call her?" Merle asks. Her hands are fists at her sides. "Now?"

"She may not come," I say, knowing that she will.

"Merle, this is crazy. You know damn well that . . ." Marshall begins. I think that now he believes in the bear.

"Then we haven't lost anything," she says.

"If she comes, we may lose," I say.

"What will we lose?" she asks. I am silent. I look at Marshall and he shrugs. "Call her," Merle says.

I stand by the fire and I call out in the Old Tongue to the spirit of the bear. Once, I call. Then I turn to Merle and say, "She does not come."

"Call again," she says.

I shrug. Once again, I call out into the night where the dire-wolves run and the saber-toothed cats stalk their prey. Again, I turn to Merle. "Again," she growls. I call again—softly and hopelessly, for I know that the bear is coming.

She sits at the fire, raindrops sparkling in her fur. She grins and her teeth shine.

"She is here," I say softly.

"Ask her if she brought in the rain and the bad luck," Merle says.

I ask and the bear laughs, shaking her head up and down, up and down. She brought the rain; she brought ill luck; she made the winds blow.

Merle frowns when I tell her. "How can I deal . . . how can I fight? . . ." she mutters. "Ask her what I can do so that she will leave us in peace to finish the film. A few days of sunshine, a few days of luck."

I ask the bear and she looks at Merle and at Marshall with arrogant eyes. She growls in the Old Tongue that the woman must leave the Valley when she has done. By the next full moon, she must be gone. She must stay away from the Valley forever. "And if she will not go?" I ask. The bear laughs. The woman can stay, but as long as the magic boxes are in the Valley, the rain will stay, the deer will run, the winds will blow, the bad luck will remain.

I look at the grinning jaws of the bear—mean, unpredictable, trickster spirit. Merle can stay—or finish and go: I look at Merle. She is of my tribe now; she must stay in the Valley. I tell her what the bear has said. "But you may stay," I say. "You may choose to stay."

Merle's eyes are large and dark; they catch the light of the fire and glow red in the darkness. Like the eyes of an animal outside the circle of light. "To finish, I must leave forever?" she says.

"That's stupid," Marshall interrupts angrily. "What are you going to do—make a promise that you'll leave, to something you can't even see?" She looks at him for a moment, her eyes on the claws that dangle from his neck. I do not speak. She may choose to stay.

"Tell her that I will go by the next full moon," she says. "And tell her that I keep my word."

The bear throws back her head to laugh and the firelight is red on her teeth and red in her eyes. And her grunting laughter lingers when the spirit fades. Laughter on the wind that blows the rain away.

Merle's hands are still fists. "I'm sorry, Sam," she says. "I'm sorry." And somewhere, the bear laughs.

The sky clears; the sun shines; the cameras run smoothly. The deer run no farther than deer should run. On one twilight evening, wolves pass by the camp, chase the deer, and bring down a fawn. Hyenas follow the pack, and fight for a share of the kill. Tim

171

says the light is good enough; he says he has it all. And long into the night, he plays the guitar and sings songs about women and drink.

It is a strange time. Merle laughs and jokes when she talks with Tim, and stops when she catches my eye. And the moon is smaller each night. Merle watches me with worried eyes. I help as I can—I show them how I chip stone for a spearhead, how I scrape the wood smooth for the shaft of the spear, how I call rabbits from hiding with whispering sounds, how I catch the fire with bow and tinder. Around me, Merle and the others move like hunters. I sit by Marshall at the fire each night and sleep alone beneath the overhanging rock.

Then there is no moon. The sky is filled with stars and the moon is gone. Soon, it will grow again, until it is full.

The fire burns late that night. I can hear Marshall and Merle talking, see the red light of the flames flare and die.

Merle is waiting for me at the spring when the sun rises. Her eyes are dark smudges; her face is pale, marked by a streak of soot across one cheek. "I wanted to talk," she says.

"Talking will change nothing," I say.

"But I wanted you to understand. . . ."

"I cannot understand," I say. I look into her dark eyes that will go away forever and I turn away. I will not talk in the slippery words of these people. I will not believe that I understand, then learn that I am wrong. I thought that she would be one of my tribe— yet she chooses to go away. I walk away into the meadow.

I see the deer far across the valley. I leave my spear and my knife by the flat rock. I go to join them as I have gone before. I go to become a part of the herd— an old buck who has a place here.

They run from me. They run—and I can smell on

myself the scent of tobacco and ashes and wine. My feet are clumsy in the grass. For a time, I run after them. I cannot run with them; I am not one of them. I run after—but I stumble on the uneven ground and I fall. They leave me behind and I lie in the grass and listen to the sound of their hooves, running away. I lie in the grass by the side of the mountain and wait, though I do not know why I am waiting.

I smell tobacco burning and I look up onto the slope of the mountain. Tim sits alone on the slope above the meadow, smoking a pipe and looking away into the distance.

"Hello, Sam," he says when I walk toward him. He offers me the pipe, but I shake my head. I sit beside him. He studies my face. "I'll tell you, Sam," he says, "don't even try to figure Merle out. She looks at the world from a different angle."

I do not speak. I am cold and the sunshine on my back does not warm me.

"She grew up independent, alone. I don't think she ever changed, really," he says. "Even when she's part of a group like this one, she's alone."

We watch the sun rise higher. The hawks soar overhead; deer graze in the meadow below us. I wonder how these deer would look through Tim's camera. Are they different from the deer that ran with me before Merle came to learn of my Valley? Or am I different? Has my world changed?

The Valley was quiet then and I was at peace. The Valley is quiet now.

At last, Tim stands. "Will you come back with me?" he asks. I shake my head. He touches my hand in farewell and walks away across the meadow.

I go to the mountains where I cannot smell the smoke of the fire or the gas of the camp stove. I fast. I watch the sunrise and the moonrise and I do not speak. From the mountain, I can see the camp.

173

The sun shines on me; the wind blows on me; I wait and I do not know why I am waiting.

I hear their voices one day, floating up the mountain. "Sam. Hey, Sam." I smell burning tobacco and I see Chris—lanky and quiet—followed by Pam, wandering through the bush. The cigarette that dangles from Chris's mouth leaves a trail of smoke behind.

And the moon is growing—from a sliver to the shape of the fruit they call the lemon. Almost full. This night, I go near enough to the camp to see the light of the fire and smell the woodsmoke. The guitar—I hear the guitar. Tim is playing softly. I hear the murmur of voices.

I stay downwind of the fire and I creep close enough to see them. Merle sits beside Marshall. Her eyes are dark shadows in the firelight.

I sleep not far from the camp, hidden in the rocks. At dawn, I hear them moving—packing boxes, cases, cameras, round, flat cans of film. When I hear the sound of the 'copter, I leave. I go to the mountain—to the cave of the bear. From the slope of the mountain, I watch them load the 'copter with all the hard and shiny things that do not belong in this Valley. Just as I do not belong outside this Valley. I recognize Tim— the tallest of them. He raises a hand, waving in farewell toward the mountains. I recognize Marshall; he does not wave and I know he will be back.

I watch the 'copter fly over the mountains and away. Still, I wait. It is not done. I wait by the cave of the bear, where the skull stares down at me.

I catch Merle's scent on the wind before I see her.

She has never been here before. She has tracked me from the Valley over the cold stone of the slope to this place.

At her side hangs the stone blade that I gave her long ago. Her head is high and her hands are relaxed at her sides. The empty eyes of the bear's skull watch her. I wait by the cave and the bear spirit stands beside me. Merle watches me.

The bear says that she is a fool. I say that she is not.

Merle watches my face. "You speak to the bear," she says. "What does she say?"

"She says you are a fool. I say you are not," I say.

She frowns. "The bear is probably right," she says.

She takes the stone blade from the thong at her side and holds it out to me. "I brought this back. I thought that I shouldn't keep it. I'm running away from the Valley. So I thought . . ."

"How is the film?" I ask.

She looks startled, then nods. "Good. I'll be editing for a while. But I am sure that we have the film."

I look at her—small woman, quick like a fox, different from my people—so different. "You must keep the knife," I say. "I do not understand you. I do not understand my brother Marshall. I see you only here." I hold up my hands in a square like the screen of the movie. "I see this much. But there is more than that I do not see. You see this much of me—no more." I shrug. "But still, you are my sister."

She hangs the knife back at her belt. Her eyes are brighter than they should be. And I know that she wishes the world fit into the frame she drew when she fought on the streets. Just as I wish the world was as I once thought it was.

I take her in my arms and hug her as I would hug a child who was hurt. And at the Barrier, I lift my hand to wave good-bye.

And I am alone.

I am always alone.

A month passes. The grass grows back where the film crew trampled it down.

Another month passes.

On a sunny afternoon I see a man, high on the

mountain slope. I recognize Marshall's red jacket. Marshall comes down the mountain slowly, like a man who is not sure of his welcome. He calls "Hello!" from high on the slope, but it is a cautious kind of greeting.

I meet him in the meadow. He stops a few steps away from me. I must step forward to clap my hands on his shoulders in greeting. "Marshall," I tell him, "I am glad you are here. I wondered when you would come."

He is studying my face, unsure of himself. "I wasn't sure you'd be glad."

I shake my head. "We are still brothers."

He walks with me to the flat rock. We sit together and I listen to him talk awkwardly about things that do not matter: the business, the Outside world.

"Tim said that he wanted to come and visit, if you would have him," Marshall says.

"I would be glad of it. He can hunt with me."

"Okay," he says. "I wasn't sure. The way you went off during the filming ..." He shrugs. "You don't understand us and sometimes I don't understand you."

"How is the film?" I ask him.

"Almost done," he says. "Keith says it'll be a classic. Tim swears it's the best he's done."

"What does Merle say?"

He hesitates, and I wonder when the time will come that I will not have to tell Marshall that he must speak to me. I touch him on the shoulder and say, "You have something to tell me. Tell me now."

"Merle and I are getting married," he says softly.

I know only a little about this custom they call marriage. I know that it means one man and one woman live together and have children.

"I came to invite you to the wedding," he says. "I want you to come and Merle wants you to come. She asked me to tell you that she wants you to come."

I stand and turn away from him, looking at the tall mountains. I am safe, here in my Valley. I am alone with the beasts. I do not want to leave this place, not now. I need to stay here and run with the deer. I belong to this place and I need its comfort. I do not want to see Merle on the Outside when I know that she should be here.

"Look, Sam." Marshall stands behind me and puts a hand on my shoulder. "Merle cares about you. She wants to see you. But she won't come back to the Valley. I asked her and . . ."

I turn to face him then. "She cannot come back to the Valley," I say. Even to my own ears, I sound harsh. "She made a bargain with the bear. She must keep it. She cannot come back."

Marshall shakes his head and scowls. "Right," he says. He is angry. He paces away from me, and turns back to face me, still scowling. "Right. She said the same thing."

"She understands," I say. "She knows."

"Damn her and damn you, Sam. You're both crazy. I don't see . . . I mean, I see why you believe in this spirit, but I don't see why Merle . . ." He turns and paces again.

He is so sure. He is so angry and so sure. He thinks that he is strong and he needs to be protected from his own certainty.

"Look," he says. He raises a hand to the claws around his neck. "If I were to take these off . . ."

"No," I say.

"Now, listen. If I were to take these off . . ." He begins to lift them from around his neck. The sun is low in the sky and our shadows are dark on the grass. His shadow changes now—darkness rising from darkness—and the she-bear stands in the grass. She is laughing.

"No," I say, and I leap at Marshall, catching the hand that touches the claws and tripping Marshall so that he falls back in the grass. I am on him and I have a grip on his hands. He bucks to throw me off, but he is winded from the fall and I am strong.

"God damn it," he is cursing. "Sam, will you? . . . Damn you." He twists beneath me and his face is in the grass, but he cannot get free. I let him swear into the grass. I hold him until he lies quiet. He lies still for a moment, then begins to struggle again.

I say to him quietly, "God damn you, Marshall. The bear is waiting for you." I jerk my head in the direction of the laughing bear spirit. "Right there. Just because you cannot see her does not mean she is not there." I hold him still. "This is my world," I say. "I understand it. Accept that." He is lying quietly again.

"Will you let me up?" he asks. His voice is muffled by the grass.

"You must promise me that you will wear the claws whenever you are in the Valley," I say.

"You're crazy, Sam."

"No," I say. "You must promise."

"What'll you do if I don't? Hold me here forever?"

He sounds more like my brother now. More like the young man I hunted with. "You still walk like a moose," I say. "I walk like a moose in the city; you walk like a moose here. Give me your word as my brother that you will wear the claws."

"I'll wear the claws," he says. "You have my word."

I let him up. He is still grumbling, rubbing loose the grass that has stuck to his face, tucking in his shirt, brushing grass from his clothes. "You and Merle," he is saying. "You're both . . ." He is shaking his head still, but his scowl has changed.

"We are trying to protect you," I say, but he keeps shaking his head.

"You're both bats," he says. "Crazy. Nuts." He has finished brushing himself off. He stands with his hands in his pockets, studying me. He looks a little worried, a little amused. "Why'd you knock me over?"

"She . . ." I start to point to the bear, but she is

178

gone. "The bear was ready for you," I say. "I could not let her take you."

"Huh," he says. He does not accept what he cannot see. "Will you come to the wedding?"

I shake my head. "I cannot."

He shrugs, still studying me. "But it's all right between us."

"You will wear the claws?"

He nods.

"You will come and hunt with me?"

Again, he nods, smiling a little.

"Then all is well."

We smoke a pipe together, but there is little left to say. "Wish Merle well for me," I tell him. "Tell Tim to come and hunt."

"I will."

We say good-bye and he promises to come back for a week after the wedding. I watch him climb the mountain into the fading light of sunset and I wish him well.

One month after Marshall's visit, I return to my hut to find Tim waiting for me. He has brought tobacco, wine, and his guitar. He brings greetings from Keith and Chris and Pamela and he has news of Merle. "Merle's pregnant," he tells me as we sit in the sunshine. "She seems pretty happy about it."

"That is good," I say. "I am glad. Merle will have a strong child."

Tim shrugs. "I can't see her settling down as a mother, but she seems happy. I suppose the kid will be a good fighter, at least." He puffs on the pipe and looks off at the hills. "Merle told me about her deal with the bear. I guess it worked. The movie looks great." He looks at me. "You'll come to the premiere?"

I shake my head. I do not want to leave the Valley now. I do not want to leave this place that is my own.

179

He does not try to convince me to come. He nods. "I'll let you know how it goes."

"You must stay and hunt with me," I say, and he agrees.

Time passes. Tim comes with reviews of the movie—almost all good. Marshall comes with news that Merle has borne a healthy baby girl. Sometimes, Tim brings Pamela or Chris with him; sometimes, he brings magazines with pictures of the Valley and of me, taken from the movie. He reads me words that tell of my life in the Valley. Time passes; season follows season. I follow the way of the shaman. Much of the time, I am alone.

4

The Shadows Are Always

13

Eighteen winters and eighteen summers have come and gone since Merle left my Valley. I know this Valley now—every rock and every tree. I have not left the Valley in all those years.

The years run together in my memory. I must think for a time to remember if the snow was deepest three winters ago or six winters ago. Was it the spring seven years ago or eight years ago that I painted a cave with hidden signs of power to make the rains come? Was it nine summers ago or ten that Tim stayed in the Valley for two months? I remember some times well; others, not at all. Tim came to visit and hunt with me often. He taught me things I did not know— things like how to take clay from the river and make pots, how to make tea from certain leaves.

Marshall came to visit often in the early years. He visited less as time passed. His trips to the moon were more frequent and, each time he left, he was away longer. Each time he returned, he spoke more of business and less of the Valley and less of Merle and her daughter, Kirsten. Five winters ago I asked him about Merle and his face reddened. "I haven't seen her for a while," he said and he avoided my eyes. "We've separated." When I frowned, he explained that they did not live together anymore, they had moved apart.

During my time alone I have explored my own powers as a shaman. As a hunter makes his tools, so does a shaman make and gather his tools. I made a shaman's cloak of deerskin. I learned the plants that are useful for visions. I wore out my first drum and made a second drum.

Through visions, I have learned the ways of the beasts, flown with the ravens, prowled the mountains with the cave lion, crept through the brush with the rabbits.

I am thirty-seven-years old—an old man by the standards of my people.

In the fall of the eighteenth year, Tim comes to me, bringing news of Roy Morgan. "He wants to come to see you," Tim says. "He says he needs to talk to you."

"What does he need to talk about?" I ask.

Tim shrugs. "He wouldn't say. Apparently he asked Marshall to bring him here and Marshall refused."

"Bring him," I say. Roy Morgan can do nothing to hurt me now and I am curious to see what he wants.

Morgan comes with Tim on his next visit. I see them far away, hiking down the mountain. Tim's red shirt is bright against the rock. As Morgan walks across the meadow toward my hut, he looks around and I wonder if he is thinking of the time when this Valley was his.

"Hello, Sam," he says to me.

I do not speak. I study his face. It is lined and weathered, but his eyes are calm. He is at ease with himself and his world. Though his hair is graying at the temples, he stands straight. He is confident and strong.

"The Outreach has succeeded," he says and he smiles. "It took longer than I thought it would, but we've found another world to hunt in."

I remember when he first told me that he would find a new world. I had to return to the Valley to make peace with the bear. But even now, I cannot leave this place. The she-bear still roams the Valley and I cannot leave this capricious spirit alone to do mischief. I cannot leave.

I shrug. "I told you long ago that I had no need of a new world."

"I thought you might have changed your mind."

I shake my head. "I will stay in the Valley."

Morgan looks up at the mountains. "We leave in spring," he says. "If you change your mind."

Through the long winter I think about this new world. I do not change my mind; I cannot change my mind. I must stay in the Valley with the she-bear. But by late spring, when the grass has grown tall and green, I am restless. Lately, my sleep has been disturbed by uneasy dreams. They are not true vision dreams that tell of a certain future. They are dreams of uncertainty and unease.

The bear spirit has been sniffing around my hut for the past three nights. I do not know what she wants; she does not speak to me. But I can smell her on the night wind. I think a change is coming.

I do not care what the bear wants. When I was younger, I would have brewed the shaman's drink so that I could chase her into her own world and make her speak to me. But I am old, and a little tired of her growling. We share the Valley and there is peace between us. That is enough.

On this day, I sit on the flat rock in the meadow and I chip a spearhead from flint. I still make weapons the way my people made them; I am still a hunter. But often now I use my rifle, rather than the spear.

The sunshine warms me, and for a moment, I put my work aside. I look out at my Valley and the tall mountains. High on the slope of the mountain, on the path from the Outside, I see two spots of color, moving slowly. A shout echoes across the Valley—"Hello, Sam!" —and I recognize the voice. Marshall has come back to my Valley. Someone is with him, but I cannot tell who it is.

184

I stand and wait for him by the flat rock. As I have grown older, I have learned a use for dignity—it saves energy. I do not run to meet my brother.

A woman walks at Marshall's side. She is young, scarcely more than a girl. Her hair is dark and she wears it in a single braid that hangs down her back. She is alert—glancing to the sky at the call of a raven, keeping an eye on the deer who graze on the far side of the meadow.

Marshall has lost weight since the last time we hunted together. He has come back from the Belt not long ago—I can tell by the way he walks. He walks as if the ground might move beneath his feet.

He claps his hands on my shoulders and grins at me. The three bear claws hang from the thong around his neck and I am glad of that. His face is thin and pale and his eyes are tired. "You're smart to stay in the Valley," he says to me. "I'm glad to be back."

"I am glad you are here," I say.

There is a tension beneath his smile that was not there when last I saw him. He swings his pack to the ground and puts his arm around the woman.

Her eyes are dark—even darker than Merle's eyes. I know before Marshall speaks that this is Merle's child. She is eighteen years old—one year younger than I was when I met Merle.

"This is my daughter, Kirsten," Marshall says. "Kirsten, this is Sam."

She holds out her hand and her eyes meet mine. She is young but she has the eyes of a shaman. A feeling of power surrounds her.

"We are here to hunt," Marshall says abruptly. "I want to hunt the cave bear." His eyes are troubled and I know that he too remembers when we first met and he said that he wanted to hunt with me.

Now I understand that the she-bear spirit has been waiting for the hunt. "It is a bad time to hunt, brother," I say. "See how tall the grass is. It is too late in

185

the spring to hunt the bear—she will not be sleeping soundly."

"We hunted once before in the late spring." The tension beneath Marshall's smile has increased.

"We were young and foolish then."

"We can be young and foolish again."

"We can be foolish," I say.

"We must hunt." There is an undercurrent of fear in his voice. "If you don't want to hunt with me, I'll hunt alone."

"Why do you want to hunt the bear?" I ask.

He shakes his head and does not answer. "The moon's full tonight," he says. "We can roll the bones and let the spirits decide. If they say the hunt will go well, we will hunt."

Marshall still does not believe in the spirits. He believes in what he calls the laws of probability. I know that he hopes that the laws will be in his favor tonight.

"We will roll the bones," I agree, admitting defeat. The mood that is upon him makes argument difficult. "We will let the spirits decide."

We sit on the flat rock and smoke the tobacco that Marshall brought for me. He talks about the Outside, but says nothing important. He is quieter than usual and I catch him gazing across the Valley, his eyes focusing on nothing. Kirsten does not sit with us. She explores along the edge of the meadow. I watch her. She moves as Merle moved—quick and restless.

At dusk, I go to hunt for our dinner. I take Kirsten with me and leave Marshall to set up their camp.

The insects in the tall grass call to each other in shrill voices as Kirsten and I follow the stream around the edge of the meadow. We walk in silence, except for the sound of Kirsten's pants legs brushing against the tall grass. She walks softly, just as her mother did.

"My mother asked me to give you her greetings," Kirsten says.

I nod, glad to hear of Merle. "She is well?"

"She's fine." Kirsten looks at the world around her as we walk. Birds fly from the grass before us; a rabbit breaks cover as we approach. She is strong and confident, like Merle. But Merle looked at the world with the eyes of a hunter. This woman is not a hunter.

"Why don't you ever leave this Valley?" she asks.

"I do not belong out there," I say. "I live here now."

"Do you ever wish you could go back to your old world?" she asks softly.

I shrug. "I could not," I say. "Time flows only forward. Even Roy Morgan could not send me back."

"But would you want to go back?"

I consider her question. I have learned to live without the comfort and strength of my tribe. I have become a shaman with no shaman to guide me. I have spoken with the Animal Master and run with the deer. I know my own power. I do not know how I would fit with my tribe now.

"I came to this place and I changed to fit this world. I live here now. The Valley is enough for me."

She is watching me closely. It has been many years since I met a new person. "My father says you are younger than he is. You look older."

I shrug. "In my tribe, I would be an old man. The shaman was the oldest man in the tribe and he had only forty winters."

She hesitates, then says, "My father is afraid he is getting old. I think that's why he wants to hunt again."

"He is old," I say. "I am old." I still do not understand these people. Though Marshall and I are blood brothers, I do not understand him.

She shrugs. "It's different for him. He wants to hunt and prove something. To himself, I think." We walk beside the stream. She watches the world carefully as she walks. "I dreamed about this place," she says. "And I asked Merle to bring me here, but she wouldn't. So I asked my father."

"What did you dream?"

She looks vaguely troubled. "I don't remember it all. I remember walking up the slope of the mountain. I remember being very happy and very unhappy. And I remember a bear, larger than any bear I've ever seen." She stops talking and frowns.

We walk close by the stream and a mist rises from the water. The mist becomes thicker and darker—and the great she-bear paces at Kirsten's side. The spirit nuzzles the woman's hair and snuffles on her neck, but Kirsten walks on, unaware of the beast looming over her. I stop, watching the woman and the bear. Though Kirsten has the eyes of a shaman, she does not see. Her power is unfocused.

The spirit moves closer to Kirsten. "This one is mine," she growls in the Old Tongue. I read trickery and deceit in her eyes. Though we have a truce, she is still a capricious spirit—sometimes generous, sometimes vindictive, but always dangerous.

Kirsten frowns at me, not knowing why I have stopped walking.

I glare at the she-bear and say in the Old Tongue, "You overstep yourself, Great One."

"I made no bargains with this one," the spirit growls. "I will take her when I am ready."

"No," I say. "She is not for you."

"We will see," the spirit grumbles. "Soon, we will see."

"Who are you talking to?" Kirsten asks. She is looking at the place the bear stands and she is frowning. "What are you saying?"

The spirit dissolves into mist before I can speak to her again. Kirsten repeats, "Who are you talking to?"

"The cave bear was following you," I say. "You did not see her."

She looks as doubtful as her father looked when I first told him that I must ask the spirits for permission to hunt. "Your father does not see the spirits," I tell Kirsten. "He does not believe in them. But you have the eyes of a shaman. You do not know your own power."

She looks around her, studying the grass and the stream. She is still frowning. "I don't see any spirit."

"She is gone," I say.

"I didn't see anything," she insists. She follows me as I walk beside the stream. "I really didn't see . . ."

I motion her to silence, because we are close to the herd of wild swine. A barrier of brush stands between me and the herd. I motion Kirsten to stay where she is and I stalk closer. The beasts raise their heads as I come near, but they do not run. In the Old Tongue, I call to them, asking one to die. An aged boar shakes his head and steps toward me. Muttering an apology for the use of the rifle, I lift the weapon and kill him with a single shot. The rest of the herd breaks and runs at the sound.

Kirsten follows me to the kill. "What did you call out just before you fired?" she asks.

"I asked which beast wanted to die." Kneeling by the boar's side, I untie the obsidian knife from the thong at my side. The boar's tusks are strong; his shoulders are broad. His spirit will help me in the coming hunt. I slit the beast's throat. My shadow on the grass shifts and changes and the boar spirit rises from the darkness and stares at me with ferocious eyes. The spirit stamps its feet in the grass and nuzzles its dead body.

"Can you see the boar's spirit there in the grass?" I ask Kirsten.

She glances at me, follows my eyes, and shakes her head. "All I see is grass. If my father doesn't see these spirits, why do you think I can?"

The spirit glares at me and I call to it in the Old Tongue. It charges but I am ready. The battle is silent; the spirit roars within me. It stamps its feet, but I surround it, holding it close as a mother holds a child.

I open my eyes and Kirsten is standing before me. She looks puzzled, worried, and she asks hesitantly, "What were you doing?"

"I have taken the spirit of the boar. When you kill a beast, you must take the spirit. Or the spirit will take you. Your father does not understand that." I stop, still clutching the obsidian blade, my hand sticky with blood.

"You really believe that?" she asks and her voice is young.

I shrug. "The spirits are all around us. How could I not believe?" I shoulder the carcass and we start back to the hut in silence.

"What did the bear spirit say to you?" she asks.

"She says that you are hers."

We walk in silence. When we are a short way from the hut, she speaks again. "Don't tell my father about this, all right?"

"It would not matter," I say. "Your father does not believe in spirits."

When we reach the hut, Marshall helps me hang the boar to bleed while Kirsten sets up their shelter. Marshall talks as he works, about his life on the Outside. Though he does not say so, I know that he has not been happy during the past few years.

"Kirsten and I are finally trying to get to know each other again," he says. "I've been gone so much these last ten years. Merle and I . . . Merle and I have been living separately and I haven't seen that much of Kirsten. But I wanted you to meet Kirsten. I wanted her to know the Valley."

"She looks like Merle," I say.

"A little," he agrees. "She's a little wild, like Merle was. She knows the streets too well for a kid so young." He shakes his head, frowning. "I worry about her."

I watch Kirsten setting up the shelter and beside her, the she-bear walks. "Do you see the gray shadow beside your daughter?" I ask him. He squints in Kirsten's direction, then shakes his head. "The bear spirit has claimed Kirsten for her own," I continue. "She is following your daughter."

"Sam . . ." he begins, but I interrupt.

"Just because you cannot see the spirit, do not deny that it is here," I say. I have grown more impatient as I have grown old.

"Look," Marshall says. He lifts the bear claws from around his neck and holds them in one hand. The she-bear spirit looks toward us with interest. "You said that these would protect me from the spirit. I'll give them to Kirsten."

"Put them back on," I say sharply. Years have passed since I knocked Marshall down and made him promise to wear the claws whenever he is in the Valley. But I will knock him down again if he does not wear them. "Put them on now." The spirit is shambling toward us. "You need them. Your daughter is strong. I can teach her to protect herself."

The spirit pauses as Marshall slips the thong back over his head. The she-bear turns and goes back to Kirsten.

"She is like Merle," I say softly—partly to Marshall and partly to myself. "Kirsten will learn."

That evening, we eat roast meat and drink the wine that Marshall brought in from the Outside. When Kirsten pours her wine, she spills a few drops on the ground. A gray mist swirls above the damp spot, but no spirit forms.

"You have not been talking about your business," I say to Marshall.

He shrugs and a shadow crosses his face. "I know you aren't interested in that." Kirsten is watching him. She turns away to watch the fire.

Marshall is yawning by the time the moon reaches its zenith. I pull the bones from the pouch at my side and I explain to Kirsten how they tell the way of the future. At my order, Marshall smooths the dust on the ground before him, facing toward the moon so that his shadow falls behind him. As Marshall casts the bones, I chant softly in the Old Tongue, asking the spirits whether the hunt will succeed.

The bones fall with the smooth side up—all three. "The hunt will succeed," I say. Marshall smiles at me. The flickering light of the fire catches in the wrinkles under his eyes. Though he still seems tired, some of the tension has left him.

"We'll be hiking tomorrow," he says. "We'd better turn in."

Kirsten remains by the fire. "I'll join you soon," she says. "I'm really not tired yet." The tension returns to Marshall's face. I can see the fear that Kirsten spoke of. He fears old age; he fears the passage of time; he fears . . . I think he fears change, though he has seen much change in the time I have known him. He turns away and goes to the shelter alone.

I sit by the fire and fill my pipe with the tobacco that Marshall brought for me. I puff the sweet smoke thoughtfully.

"Why did you come here?" I ask Kirsten. I need to know more about this girl–woman who does not know her own power. She reminds me of Merle. But Merle knew her own power; this child does not.

"My father asked me to come with him," she says. I wait, asking no more. She continues, after a pause, in a lower voice. "My father found something here when he was young. And my mother . . . my mother found something. I thought . . ." She breaks off her sentence and shrugs. "I don't know what I'm looking for. But I dreamed of this place and I knew I must come here."

I nod. She is much like Marshall as a youth. But he was a fighter and she has another power.

"Tell me about the spirit that was following me," she asks. "Why does it follow?"

"The she-bear follows because you are powerful, but you don't know your strength."

"I'm not powerful," Kirsten says.

"Why do you back away from your power?" I ask. When she does not speak, I continue. "The bear will come to you as the spirit of the boar came to me. Unless you recognize your power, you will not be able to fight her."

I blow a puff of smoke from my pipe at the gray mist that swirls beside Kirsten and the bulky shape of the spirit appears. She grumbles and snuffles, twitching her hairy ears and squinting her tiny eyes to gaze at me across the fire. "Look there," I say. "The spirit is back."

Kirsten stares in the direction that I am pointing. "I can't see anything."

The she-bear interrupts me, growling in the Old Tongue that I must teach Kirsten nothing—the woman is hers. I growl back, asking her if she fears a fair battle. In answer, the spirit opens her mouth and rears back to her full height, towering above the fire.

"Could my mother see the bear?" Kirsten asks.

"Merle knew the bear was here, but she never saw her. She had a different kind of power," I say.

"Some people say that I'm like my dad. Maybe that's why I can't see her."

"You will see," I say. The she-bear laughs. She shuffles a step closer to Kirsten and towers over the woman. Kirsten makes no sign that she senses the spirit's presence. "Can you see the shadow that looms above you?" I ask.

"I see moonlight and firelight," she says. But she blinks and for a moment I think that her eyes focus on the spirit. But she shakes her head in denial.

The bear laughs again and fades into the mist. Kirsten still gazes at the spot where I pointed. "She's gone," I say gently. "She will be back. I will teach you to fight her."

"I can't fight what I can't see."

"You will see her," I say. But even as I say the

193

brave words I wonder if I can teach this woman with a shaman's eyes to see what she does not want to see.

We do not begin hiking until noon the next day. The mountain is steeper now than it was when I was younger. We will camp on the mountain slope and go to the bear cave at dawn.

Marshall is alert when we begin hunting, and Kirsten watches him with concern. "He's taking stimulants," she says when Marshall is out of earshot. "He's used to lower gravity now." She shakes her head. "He can't keep this up for long."

As we start to climb higher on the mountain slope, Marshall hikes more slowly. His shoulders sag beneath the weight of the pack and he sweats more than the sun and the heat demand. "Are you well, brother?" I ask when we stop to rest.

"Of course. I'm fine," he snaps, then tries to soften his tone with a smile. "We should worry about the youngest in the group." He gestures to Kirsten, who has been carrying her pack steadily without complaint.

He walks away from me, out to the edge of the ledge where we have stopped. I see him take something from his pack and swallow it, washing it down with water from his canteen. After lunch, Marshall walks with the energy of a young man.

We make camp on the side of the mountain, atop a small rise where the trees shelter us from the wind. At the campfire, Marshall nods as he stares into the flames. The pill has worn off. "We should not be hunting this late in the year," I say to him. "We can still turn back."

"No," he says, just as stubborn now as he was as a youth. "The bones predicted success."

"Success in the hunt," I say. "But what are you hunting for?"

He stands, and his shoulders sag as if he still carried the pack. "If you turn back, I'll go on alone."

"Your daughter . . ." I begin, trying to remind him of her danger, but Kirsten interrupts.

"Not alone," she says.

He smiles at her as he turns away, a flash of teeth that makes him look almost young again. Kirsten watches him walk to the shelter and duck inside. "I can take care of myself," she says to me softly.

"You do not know how great your danger is," I say. "The spirit will take your body and leave you with nothing." But I doubt my own words as I speak. I think of Roy Morgan and the hyena spirit.

"I am different from your people. Maybe the spirit will not hurt me," she says. Her eyes are bright and she looks like Merle. Maybe this one is strong enough to bargain with the bear. Maybe. But I think that she fears to claim her power and her strength. "You could go back, Sam," she says.

I shake my head. "Marshall is my blood brother. I will stay with him."

She sits without speaking, watching the flames while the moon rises. "Let me roll the bones," she says when the moon is near the peak of its journey.

"You may not like the answer," I say, but she holds out her hand and I give her the bones.

She smooths the ground before her and casts the bones. The three bones gleam white in the moonlight: three white sides up. Success. Just outside the circle of firelight, the she-bear chuckles. I can hear her shaking her heavy head as she laughs. Kirsten does not hear. She is studying the bones.

"Success in the hunt," she says. "Now if only I knew what it is I am hunting." She gives me the bones, hesitating as she places them in my hand. "Will you roll the bones, Sam?"

I shake my head. "No. I do not seek anything now. I do not need to know what the future holds." I am old. I do not hunt now.

The next morning, the morning that we will hunt the bear, I awaken at dawn. Kirsten is awake. She stands by the burned-out fire and I watch her. She stares at the slope of the mountain above us, her hands clenched at her sides. Beside her, unnoticed, stands the she-bear.

The spirit vanishes when I approach. I touch Kirsten's shoulder but she does not look at me. Watching her set face, I remember a long-ago dawn when Marshall and I gathered brush to burn at the entrance to a she-bear's cave. Marshall had been afraid and I had been afraid. But I am no longer afraid.

I lift the bear claws from around my neck and place them around Kirsten's neck. I say, "She cannot touch you now. You are safe."

She raises a hand and runs a finger along the curving length of one claw. Her expression is a strange mixture of fear and anticipation, relief and a kind of regret. "She can't touch me, but what about you?"

"I have hunted the bear before. She does not want me. She wants you."

"My father . . ." she begins.

I interrupt. "Your father will not be able to keep you safe from something he does not believe in."

She falls silent for a moment, then says, "I'm afraid for you and for my father."

"We will take care of ourselves," I say. She raises her hand again to touch the bear claw and feel the sharp tip.

Together, we gather brush for the fire we will light by the bear's cave. "What did my father find here when he hunted the bear with you?" she asks.

"I am not sure," I say slowly. "He found his father's pride, and that was important. He found a kind of strength."

"I wonder what I will find," she mutters.

At breakfast, Marshall is quiet. If he notices the bear claws around his daughter's neck, he does not comment. He checks his rifle once, twice, three times, and tests the edge of the spear I have given him.

I carry the bundle of brush as we climb the granite slope of the mountain, following the path that twists around boulders and along narrow ledges. Marshall and I have talked and argued and decided on the plan of the hunt. I will light a fire to drive the bear from the cave. I will stand on one side of the ledge and Marshall will stand—rifle and spear ready—at the other side of the ledge. Kirsten will wait on the ledge above the cave, a rifle in hand. She knows how to shoot, Marshall says. He taught her long ago.

I follow Marshall along the narrow path to the cave. I remember this place well. The ledge in front of the cave mouth is not much larger than the floor of my hut. The ledge ends in a sheer drop; jagged rocks lie below. The wind that swirls in and out of the cave carries the scent of bear.

I build the fire quietly. As I light it, I hear the sound of movement within the cave. I run to my spot, waving to Marshall to tell him. "She is coming." I whirl to face the entrance, holding my spear ready. I hear the bear behind me.

She is fast, too fast for a sleepy bear. As she charges, I dodge to one side, ducking a halfhearted swing of her paw. She is turning toward Marshall. He is shouting curses at the beast, shouting over the sound of her roar.

The animal is full-grown, almost the size of the bear spirit. Even on all fours, she is Marshall's height. Roaring, she rises on her hind legs.

The wind changes and the pungent smoke of the fire surrounds us. There is smoke and the roaring of the bear. There is smoke, there is shouting, there is confusion, there is a gray mist through which I start to step to go to the aid of my brother.

197

But the mist becomes solid. The she-bear spirit stands before me, blocking my path. I know this spirit, but her eyes gleam with a new light. She swats at me with a paw, but I duck back. I am on the edge of the cliff and there is nowhere to run. She grins at me as she rears back on her hind legs.

"Sam!" I hear a shout from above. The spirit looks up and the bear claws that Kirsten throws to me rattle against the stone at my feet. Even before I snatch them up, the spirit is gone. I turn and see the girl–woman on the ledge above me, facing a shadow that looms over her.

Marshall shouts and I look to him. The bear has him. He is on the edge of the cliff. His rifle lies several feet away and he holds only his spear. As the bear swings a paw at him, he thrusts with the spear, missing the bear but ducking away from a sweeping blow of her paw. He smiles as he did when he was young— old eyes burning with a new flame. Joyous. The wrinkles are gone from his face; his eyes are clear. I start toward him, then hesitate.

From the ledge above, I hear Kirsten's voice. She calls to me in the Old Tongue, in a voice of power that stops me. She grins down at me. I can see in her eyes both woman and bear. The bear spirit grins—sometimes vindictive, sometimes generous, sometimes angry, sometimes compassionate.

I look to Marshall. Kirsten could shoot now. The she-bear within her could turn the bear away from her father. Marshall shouts at the animal and thrusts again with the spear. He wears the look of a man who is meeting death as he wants to meet it. The bear towers over him, hesitating.

Sometimes compassionate.

The bear's paw sweeps down in a blow that catches Marshall and tumbles him off the cliff. Even as he falls and the bear turns away, Kirsten is scrambling down from her ledge, almost falling, stumbling, almost running. She rushes down the slide of loose rock to the base of the cliff, slipping with the shifting talus, almost falling, catching herself—clumsy, quick, powerful, graceful woman–bear–girl. I follow more slowly, picking my way down the slope.

Kirsten stands over her father's body, fists clenched. A thin trickle of blood flows from a scrape on her arm where she fell against a boulder. She looks up when I approach and I can see the wild flicker in her eyes: woman–bear–girl–bear. "I could have stopped the bear," her voice stammers softly. "I met the spirit and she ... and I ... we ..." She growls in the Old Tongue the word for merging, for union, for when two streams join to make a river. "I knew then that I could stop ..." Words catching, halting, beginning again. "I could have ... but it was better that ... better, but I could have stopped ..." Her eyes fill with tears, but the wild changes—woman–bear–girl–bear—do not stop and her fists do not relax. I reach out and touch her shoulder and the tears spill over. For a moment a fearful child, Merle's own daughter, peers from the dark pools where she mourns for Marshall. "He's dead, Sam. Do you think he wanted to die?" Tears spill and she kneels by her father's battered head. I stand with my hand on her shoulder; I understand now why she had feared her power. I understand, but that changes nothing.

We leave the bear claws around his neck and we leave his rifle and his spear at his side. We build a cairn, Kirsten and I, rolling and carrying rocks to surround him, to pile over him, to keep back the animals and to protect him. I do not know who I will see each time I look at Kirsten—woman, bear, or girl–child.

When we finish, Kirsten stands over the mound of rocks. Her hands are scratched and bruised, but they are relaxed now. "I wonder if he truly wanted what he found here," she murmurs. "I wonder if he is happy now."

I have no answers for her. We make the journey back to my hut. We walk together quietly and, as we walk, she becomes more at ease with herself. I can see it in the way she walks and the way she looks at me and the soft sound of her voice when she asks me for a drink of water. Her eyes are calmer.

She tells me that I must continue to wear the bear claws and I nod. But I cannot tell whether the bear speaks or the woman. Perhaps both.

"Where will you go?" I ask her as we walk.

"I'm going home," she says and she only hesitates a moment before she says home. "Back to the city."

"What will you do there?" I ask her.

She looks puzzled, worried. She wets her lips before she speaks. "I don't know." Her voice is low. "I'm not . . . there's something to be done there. I'm not sure what, but I have to go."

What will she do? Will she speak to Merle? Will she watch the humans and laugh—large, compassionate, vindictive, angry? Will she seek out Roy Morgan? I do not know what the shaman–woman–bear–girl–child will do. But I am old and I am tired and I will not stop her.

At my hut, she turns to the Outside. She looks back at me and the dark-eyed child looks out of her eyes. "Come with me, Sam."

I shake my head. I do not belong in the Outside. I belong here in the Valley. "I will not go," I say. "But I wish you good luck."

She smiles tentatively. It is a small smile, but it carries hints of great wickedness, hints of great joy and great sorrow.

"Did I do right, Sam?" she asks me.

"You did what you had to do," I say. "You did well." I can see the girl–child peering out from her eyes and

200

I say, "I will not come with you, but you must come back to the Valley. Come back to visit."

She frowns. "No, Sam. The time for that is done. I am going home." I cannot tell who speaks, the woman or the bear. She turns away.

She walks toward the Outside, casting a shadow larger than herself.

14

Marshall is dead. Kirsten is gone from the Valley. And Amanda—*dark* never returned to me.

I roam the Valley alone, trying to live as I have always lived. But the Valley is not the same. I am uncomfortable now, restless and unhappy.

I fast; I go to the sweathouse. And at last I brew the shaman's drink from the leaves and the flowers of the shaman's plant. The taste of the drink is bitter. Clear water does not wash the taste away, the bitterness remains at the back of my throat.

The Valley changes then. Suddenly, this is a bigger and brighter world. The green of the meadow and the blue sweep of the sky are so bright they hurt my eyes. The mountains are taller. The water that I scoop from the stream is colder against my skin. I feel each blade of grass that brushes against me, each breeze that passes by. The Valley is bright and clear. And empty.

Empty. I sit on the flat rock and look across the Valley. I can see deer grazing in the meadow, but they do not seem real. They are like paintings on a wall of rock—they are not really here.

When a raven caws in a nearby tree, his call echoes in an empty world.

Through this empty world, a figure strides toward me. I see the Animal Master walking quickly and silently through the meadow. The deer lift their heads to watch him pass.

He stands before me, the tip of his lion tail twitching in the grass. His yellow eyes watch me steadily.

"I told you long ago that this time would come," he says in the Old Tongue. "You must help me now." He points out over the hills toward the Barrier. "You must go."

I stand and I look directly into his yellow eyes. I am as tall as the Animal Master. Once, he was taller. He has shrunk over the years. Or I have grown larger. "Where must I go?" I ask.

"You must find the man who took the hyena spirit," he says. "You must find the bear."

I am tired. I do not want to go to the Outside. "I do not have to go," I say. "You cannot make me go."

His tail twitches, brushing against the grass tops. I can hear the sound each time his tail strikes the grass. He is impatient with me.

I do not lower my gaze before him. "I do as I want," I say.

He nods slowly. "You could stay here," he says at last. "You must choose."

"What will happen if I leave the Valley?"

He shakes his head. His eyes glint gold in the sunlight. "I do not know. I do not understand everything in the Outside. I do not understand this world."

I frown at him. He spreads his claw-tipped hands before him and I recognize the golden glint in his eyes. He is laughing at himself and at me. "Times have changed," he says. "Times are changing. I do not know what will happen."

202

"It is my choice," I say.

"Your choice," he agrees, and only the tip of his tail moves.

"I will go," I say softly. "There is nothing for me here."

I speak to an empty world. The raven calls from a nearby tree and the deer lift their heads as if to watch someone pass near the herd. But no one is there.

I pack food and water in a deerskin sack. I take the leaves of the shaman's plant; I may need them. I wonder what the Outside will be like, without Marshall to help me. I wonder what Roy Morgan will say to me and I to him. I climb the mountain's slope to the Barrier. I do not look back.

The road is as I remember it. I shoulder my sack and I begin to walk in the direction of the city.

I cannot see into the cars that pass me—their windows are silver in the morning light. Each car slows a little as it passes me and speeds up after. I do not like walking here beside the moving cars, but I must go to the city and this is the way to the city.

After a time, a car pulls off the road beside me. It is a white car with a flashing light on top. The men who step out are not smiling.

I stop walking and I face them. "What seems to be the trouble?" the younger man says. "Car breakdown?"

"No," I say.

They are looking at my clothes and my pack. "Get lost in the woods?" the other asks. This one is a stocky man with gray hair.

"No," I say, wondering how a person could get lost in the woods. The cars still pass us, slowing, but never stopping.

"Well," the first man says impatiently. "You going to explain?"

I frown at him. "Explain what?"

He flashes a look at his companion and shakes his head. "What's your name?" he says to me. "Where did you come from? And why the hell are you walking down the freeway in the middle of nowhere?"

"My name is Sam," I say. "I come from the Valley. I must go to the city."

The young man frowns. "Sam what?"

"Sam," I say. "Sam is my name."

He scowls and starts to speak again but his partner lays a hand on his arm. The older man has been watching me steadily. "Now wait," he is saying. "You're Sam, the Neanderthal that the Morgan Foundation brought back."

"Yes."

"Well, look . . ." he begins, speaking to his partner. His voice drops low and he keeps a grip on the younger man's arm. The younger one studies me and frowns while his partner talks. Then the younger man goes to talk into a box in the car. "I think that we'd better take you to the city," the older man says to me. "You have friends there?"

I nod slowly. "I need to see Roy Morgan."

The man nods. "We'll take you there."

In the car, the older man talks to me. The young man drives. "I'm glad to meet you, Sam," the older man says. "My name's Chuck. I saw that film about the Valley. That bit about the wolves—hey, that was something. And the deer and . . ." He shakes his head and though he is smiling, there is a sadness around his eyes. "I must have seen the film six times. Nothing like that Valley."

His young partner is frowning. "What about the Outreach planets? If you're so hot for wildlife, why don't you just head out?" He sounds as if he has said this many times before.

"If I were a single man and if I were rich, I would," says Chuck. "I sure wouldn't stay in this place." He gestures to the road and the buildings around us. The sky overhead is gray. "If it weren't for my kids and

204

the wife and ..." His words trail off, just as they must have trailed off so many times.

He is quiet then, as we drive through the city to a place Chuck calls the Station. In the Station, a man sitting behind a desk listens while Chuck explains where they found me and who I am. He frowns at me. "You want to contact Roy Morgan?" he says.

I nod.

He shakes his head, scowling, and he mutters, as if to himself, about things not being police business, about rich men, about stupid patrolmen who ... but Chuck and his partner are carefully not listening.

The man at the desk speaks into a telephone, dials a number, and speaks again. The frown on his face fights with a look of surprise, but the frown wins. He hangs up, then says, "He'll be here. You two can get out and finish your shift."

Chuck and his partner start to turn away, then Chuck turns back. He puts his hand on my arm. "Hey, Sam," he says. "Could you? ..." He puts a pen and a piece of paper in my hand. "An autograph for my kid," he says. "He'll never believe me otherwise."

"An autograph?" I say without understanding.

"Sign your name," says the young man.

I sign my name, slowly and carefully as James Andrews taught me. Chuck grins. "Good luck," he says, and he and his partner leave.

I wait for Roy Morgan. I sit in a chair and the man sitting behind the desk taps his pen nervously. The clock on the wall clicks each time a minute passes. The man shuffles papers on his desk, looking at the papers and every minute or so, looking up at me. After the clock clicks thirty times, the phone buzzes and the man answers it, looking relieved. "Yes, send him in," he says.

I hear footsteps in the hall and I stand to greet Roy Morgan.

Roy Morgan carries himself with power and grace.

205

He smiles when he sees me. He is at ease with himself and with the world. "I'm glad you've come, Sam," he says. "Your timing is perfect. I have something to show you."

Outside the Station, rain is falling. The streets are wet and the world is streaked with gray. We drive through the city in a large black car.

The hallways of the Foundation building are white, just as white as they were when I walked here with Amanda—*dark*. Roy Morgan is silent as he leads me through these halls. When he does speak, his voice is no longer empty and hollow. When he smiles, his eyes smile too. His restlessness seems channeled now. He is waiting, as a hunter may wait for an animal to break cover. Ready and eager, but waiting.

At last, we stand before a screen—like the screen on which Amanda—*dark* showed me the Valley so long ago. The screen flickers and I see a broad plain. Green plants grow here—low plants that are not marsh plants and not grasses, but something between the two. Animals are grazing here—strange animals that are not deer and not bison and not camels. One has a hump like a bison. But the beast's snout moves like the trunk of a mammoth and the beast uses it to tear up clumps of plants to eat. A herd of animals that are not quite deer graze some distance from the not-bison. These beasts look like deer, but their heads are bony in the wrong places and their fur is the color of the marsh plants.

"It is a fine world," Roy Morgan says to me. "It would provide hunting for many tribes. But no one hunts here. Not yet." He fingers the controls beside the screen and the view changes. We are looking down on a clump of trees. A herd of the not-bison are browsing on the leaves, using their snouts to pull branches close to their mouths. "It's a new world," he says. "The best I've found. Are you coming with me?"

"Not alone," I say. And I tell him of Kirsten and the

spirit of the bear. And Merle—I think of Merle and realize that she could come with us to this new world.

"If they wish to come, they will be welcome," he says. He looks at the screen with longing. "And there will be others," he begins, then stops. "I won't tell you about that yet. There is someone else who needs to talk to you."

He leads me through the white hallways and stops at a door. He opens the door and I step inside. I hear the door close softly behind me.

"Hello, Amanda–*dark*," I say.

She is smaller than I remember her. Her eyes are more uncertain. She stands—she had been sitting on a couch. One of her hands clutches the other. I look at her face and something seems wrong. I study her for a moment and I know what it is—she has not changed. She is no older now than when she ran from my room twenty-six years ago.

"Sam?" she says hesitantly. She starts to smile, but her mouth wavers and her face seems to crumple. "Sam?"

Then my arms are around her and she is smaller than I remember—as frail as the little birds that flit through the grass in the Valley. But her scent is the same.

I feel the wetness of her tears on my chest and I stroke her thin back. I do not know what to say. At last, she looks up, and her eyes are the same dark eyes that I remember.

"I think . . ." she says, "I guess . . . I'm all right. It just seemed like . . . you're so different. Roy Morgan's so different. And suddenly, I didn't know what to say to you."

"You have not changed," I say to her. I touch her cheek—still smooth and unwrinkled. "Why did you stay away so long?"

She frowns and shakes her head. "Not so long. Not by my count. Long enough to blink." She takes one of my hands in both of hers. "Cynthia said she would send me to a time I could help you and be part of the Project again. She sent me here." Amanda—*dark* clutches my hand more tightly. "Roy Morgan was going to send me away and I had no choice. She sent me here." She is studying my face just as I am studying hers. "Your eyes are different," she says. "You look like you have been very unhappy."

"Sometimes I have been unhappy," I say. I stop, and my hands tighten on her shoulders. "I waited for you for a long time, Amanda—*dark*."

Her eyes are steady on my face. "Then you gave up waiting?"

I think for a moment, then I shake my head. "No. I stopped thinking about waiting, but I still thought you would come back."

"You speak well."

"I had a good teacher."

We sit together on the couch and we talk. Slowly, at first. I tell her about the bear and she traces the line of the scar on my leg. I tell her about Merle and she frowns and nods. I tell her about Kirsten and how I must go back to the city and find Kirsten and the bear.

Strange—I look into Amanda—*dark*'s eyes and I think of the true dream when I went back to my tribe. How different this frail-boned woman is from my mother. How different her tiny hands are from my mother's strong hands. But somehow, their eyes are the same. Amanda—*dark* watches me with pride and wonder, just as my mother watched me in the firelight of the true dream long ago.

At last, I stop talking. "You are stronger now," she says. "I wish I could have helped you when you were not so strong. I don't know if now . . ." She stops and frowns a little, as if to herself. "Do you remember when I said that I would try to send you back to your people?"

I nod.

Her eyes are focused on something far away. "I can't send you back. It can't work that way. You can only go forward. But I can bring your tribe here."

My hand is tight on her shoulder and I cannot speak. I remember when Amanda—*dark* first told me that my people were dead and gone. But maybe not gone. That could change.

"I couldn't do it without Roy Morgan's help. But he will help now." She leans back and her eyes focus on my face again. "I see your people in the past and I can see a time when they are hungry. The game animals have gone. Their world is changing. I will take them from that time."

I think of the shaman's eyes in the dim light of the place between this world and my tribe. "You must make your peace with the bear," the shaman had said.

"Yes," I say. "And they will come with us to the new world. But first, I must find the bear."

"You can," she says. She smiles at me and I think of my mother, though my mother never smiled as these people smile. "You will."

Amanda—*dark* understands that I must go away and return. Roy Morgan accepts this, too. He shows me how to use the phone to contact Merle. Merle may help me find Kirsten.

Merle is confused when I talk to her on the phone. She does not understand where I am or what I need at first. But she comes to meet me at the Foundation.

I meet her at the gate in the evening. The day has faded to twilight and the grass and trees are gray and wet. Merle's car is small and low to the ground. It has seats for two people only. I can hardly see her face in the shadowy car, but I recognize her scent. She accelerates away from the Foundation and the car skids for a moment on the wet drive. She recovers. She drives as if she were a part of the car.

"You came to see Morgan?" she asks abruptly.

"I needed to see him. But that is not the only reason I came." She glances at me quickly, then looks back at the road. I do not want to tell her all the reasons I came. Not here in this speeding car. Not yet.

"You missed the funeral," she says. "We had a closed casket ceremony for Marshall. We buried an empty casket with the pomp and ceremony befitting the end of a rich man with a famous father." The whine of the car's engine is loud. "I thought we should leave the body in the Valley. He would rather stay there, I think. Or else be jettisoned in the Belt." She does not look at me.

"He wanted to die," I say. "He was happy when he died."

She nods, her eyes on the road ahead. The rain strikes the windshield of the car and runs away in streams. "I know," she says.

I watch her face, but she does not look at me, and she does not say why Marshall wanted to die.

"Kirsten did not cry at Marshall's funeral," she says. "She has changed since she came back from the Valley."

"I know," I say, and this time she glances away from the road to look at my face.

"We'll talk when we get to my house," she says.

Merle's home is outside the city—a small house surrounded by trees. The room we enter is paneled with dark wood and lined with shelves.

I can see Merle clearly for the first time. She is older. There are dark smudges beneath her eyes and the skin of her face is creased with many tiny wrinkles. She has changed and aged just as I have changed and aged.

"Would you like some coffee? I could use a cup myself," she says.

It has been several years since I had coffee, and I nod. She goes to another room to make coffee and I wait.

I cannot sit still. I remember now how the Outside

makes me feel. I am restless, nervous. There are too many scents and sounds that are new to me. I have been alone in the Valley with the spirit of the bear for too long.

Pictures hang on the dark walls—a picture of the Valley, a picture of the pockmarked face of the full moon, a picture of Marshall and Kirsten and Merle together.

On one shelf, there are knives. One looks like the knife that Zee carried strapped to her leg and I remember Merle's film of the knife-fighters. One is the hunting knife that Merle carried when she first came to the Valley. One is the stone blade that I gave to Merle.

I pick up the shiny black stone and run my finger along the edge. It is still sharp. I hold the blade in one hand and I feel more at ease. Reluctantly, I place it back on the shelf.

I am looking at a picture of Marshall and Merle when Merle returns, carrying two steaming cups.

"That was taken several years ago," Merle says. "Back before Marshall and I separated and Kirsten moved out to go to school."

She sets the cups down on a low table and she sits on the couch. She links her hands behind her head and leans back, as if she were relaxed and at ease. But I can read the tension in her arms and the way she holds her head. She watches my face.

"Marshall and I were separated four years ago," she says. "Kirsten had moved out to go to school and we had been going in different directions before that. He would be home for a while, then off to the moon, or to the Belt or to the Valley, then he'd be back for a while. I would be off to a new location, out working in the field, pitching an idea...." She is looking into the distance now. "It almost worked," she says. "But neither of us was willing to give up our first love. My first love was my work; Marshall's first love was his father's business. The moon and the Belt and the cold, barren places there." She shakes her head. "His second love was either the Valley or Kirsten—I'm not sure which. Or both, since Kirsten was so closely linked to the Valley."

"Yes," I say. "She seemed to fit the Valley."

She studies my face, frowning. "Marshall never told you, did he? Kirsten may be your daughter. My hormone implant failed when I was in the Valley—she could be your daughter, or she could be Marshall's. Marshall and I talked about it, but decided we didn't want to know who the father was."

I shrug. "It does not matter who her father was. You are her mother and so she is of my tribe."

"Yes," she says softly. "I thought that was how it might be." She stops a moment and she looks down at her hands. "You know, I've wondered sometimes about the decision I made back in the Valley. I wonder if I decided right. Maybe I should have stayed in the Valley and let the film go. Maybe I would have been happier. Maybe Marshall would have been happier. . . ."

I sit beside her on the couch and I close my hand around her fingers. "It is done. You followed your way. Now you must go on."

She looks up and her eyes are bright. "I thought you would say that, too."

I stroke her hand and she grins at me—a shadow of her old grin. "You said that Marshall wanted to die," I say to her. "Why?"

"Ah," she says softly. "It was that first love of his— the business." I can feel the tension in her hands. "Marshall wanted the world his father built in the Belt to grow and be strong. And it did grow—for a while. But when the Outreach succeeded, the world in the Belt suddenly seemed so small, so limited, such a dead end. All that fabulous, high-technology equipment, designed for mining in the Belt and processing the ores—all of it was outmoded, since the Outreach

212

could send people across space without sending them through. And worse, the Belt was no longer the place to seek adventure. Why go to the barren reaches of the moon when you can go to another world? In a moment, the empire he built became insignificant. He could begin again, or choose not to begin again. He chose not to." She is silent again. "I didn't realize what he had chosen until Kirsten came back alone."

I nod. Marshall made his choice. The world had changed and he chose not to change.

"Kirsten had changed when she came back," Merle is saying. "She seemed stronger and sometimes, when I looked in her eyes, I didn't know her at all. She didn't cry at the funeral. She stood stiff and straight by the graveside and did not cry."

"You knew her," I say. "But she was not your daughter. Not entirely." And I tell her about Kirsten and the bear. As quickly and clearly as I can, I tell her about the Outreach and Roy Morgan and Amanda–*dark*. I tell her that the spirit of the bear must come to this new world, that Kirsten must come.

When I am done, she is frowning. "Marshall never believed in the spirit of the bear. I believed. . . ."

"And Kirsten believed," I say. "From the start, she believed."

Merle leans back on the couch. "Kirsten carries this spirit with her."

"Yes."

"And you have come to find her."

"Yes."

"What will happen when you find her?"

"I do not know. The world is changing in ways it has not changed before. New things are happening."

She studies my face. "But she will go with you to this new world."

"Kirsten will come and you will come. You are part of my tribe."

Her hand relaxes in mine and she nods. "All right. We will find her. And see what happens."

"It may not be easy," I say. "The bear is a trickster spirit."

She shrugs and reaches for the telephone. "We'll try the easy way first."

But Kirsten does not answer the telephone. Merle calls Kirsten's friends at school, but no one has seen the girl. Merle shakes her head and narrows her eyes. "She's gone to the streets, I guess. She has friends there, knows her way around." She stands—quick and graceful. "We'll go to the streets to look for her." Her eyes are alive and she is balanced lightly on the balls of her feet. She is ready—to run, to hunt, to fight.

She takes two knives from the shelf. The metal one, she straps to her leg. The stone one, she gives to me. "Best to carry some blade when you prowl the streets on a rainy night," she says. Her face seems younger now, and her mouth curves up at the corners, as though she were about to grin.

She moves quickly and I follow her.

The small car growls as we speed back to the city. The full moon has risen. It shines on the streets just as it shone on my Valley. Merle's window is open and I can smell the wet streets. The rain has stopped.

"I haven't been to the streets for a while," she says. "They speak a different cant there now. But they still watch that first film of mine—for knife technique, if nothing else." She shakes her head. Her eyes are amused, distant.

I watch her face and I frown. "You are not worried about your daughter?" I ask.

She glances at me and her face is in shadow. "Marshall once accused me of not caring about people, never worrying. He was partly right. I don't worry. When there is something to be done, I act. When I can do nothing, I do nothing." She shrugs, a movement of shadows. "That hasn't changed."

We drive in silence through streets lit only by moonlight. Most of the buildings are dark. A few people walk here—they dress in black and I can see the glint of metal on this one's leg, that one's belt. Best to carry a blade, Merle had said. They walk slowly and linger in the shadows. I do not like the shadows of this dark city.

We stop the car beside a brightly lit building and get out. I follow Merle.

"This is Corey's place," she says to me over her shoulder. "He may have seen her. Stay close."

Corey's place is crowded with people and thick with smoke and many scents. I stay close to Merle. I am as alert as I would be on a hunt. Merle nods to some of the people we pass, but only to a few.

The fragments of talk that I hear are strange. I cannot understand the meanings, though I know the words. This is a confusing place and my hand rests on my knife.

Merle leans against the long bar and I stand just behind her. ". . . looking for Kirsten," she is saying to the man behind the bar.

I do not listen. I am watching the eyes of the people who sit at the tables and lounge by the walls and crowd into shadowy booths. They remind me of something, of a time I cannot place. The door opens and, for a moment, I can smell the rain outside. The door closes and again the air in the room is still.

A young man is coming toward me, leaving his place at the wall. His eyes are bright, reflecting the lights of the bar. He is scowling and he walks with a slow and deliberate pace.

"You watch me," he says. "Why?" His hand is open, as if ready to grab a knife.

"Hey," says the man behind the counter. "Not here."

"But the man watches me like . . ." the young man begins.

"Shut it and down yourself," says the barman. "Or

I'll down you." And the light fades from the young man's eyes as he turns away.

I remember seeing eyes like his before. I remember the dire-wolf called Lobo in the cage at the Project. His eyes had glowed with the memory of the hunt. He paced in his cage, restless and trapped.

Merle's hand is on my shoulder. "I should have warned you to keep your eyes to yourself. Be careful." She turns away from the bar and I follow her. "No sign of Kirsten. We'll try elsewhere."

We go to a bar called Jarl's Place. And another called Syber's and another that has no name. I follow Merle. I do not look into the eyes of these people and I stay close to Merle.

"Not here," says the woman behind the bar in the place with no name. "If she wants to stay dark, she'll stay dark—and no one will glim her. She's no dull, that kid."

When Merle turns away, her face is tired. "She's hiding. Not just drinking and smoking, but gone to cover. Corey had seen her yesterday; Jarl, last night. But they say she was strange. Lost. Looking for fights." We walk back toward the car. "She could be with people I don't know. All we can do is try tomorrow night."

There is light in the east—dim light filtered through clouds. The air has a dangerous feel and the hairs on my arms prickle within my shirt. "The bear does not want to be found," I say.

"We'll try tomorrow," she says. "It's dawn now. And all the night people are going to ground. We won't find her now."

The cement is cold beneath my feet and the rain is cold on my skin. I have been cold and weary many times. I have been cold and wet and hungry in the Valley. But it is not just the cold that has seeped into my bones. It is the feeling of this city. The shadows are too dark. I do not like these tall gray buildings. I

216

do not like the sullen hiss of passing cars. Something hides in the shadows and I fear this place.

I see movement in the shadows, but when I look closer I see nothing. I feel the air shifting around me, restless and tense. The shaman's drink would let me see clearly into the shadows—but I do not want to see. With the shaman's drink, I could find the bear—just as a shaman can find game where no hunter can find it. But this city is a dark and dangerous place and I do not want to see it clearly.

We drive back through the dark streets. We go back to the warm house, but even here I am cold. The shadows of the street are with me, even here.

"Let's get a few hours sleep," Merle is saying. "We both need it."

The shadows are around me. I put my hands on Merle's shoulders and I say, "I do not want to sleep alone."

"Neither do I," she says.

She leads me to a large bed. She is small in the circle of my arms. She shivers and I hold her close to warm her.

It is good to hold her. Good to feel her against me—still strong and still gentle. I stroke her back and she moves closer to me. The gray sunlight filters through the window to touch the gray streaks in her hair.

She is watching my face. "What are you thinking?"

"I am thinking that there are too many shadows in the city," I say.

"Don't think about the city now," she says.

"But there are too many shadows," I say again.

"They have always been there," she says. "No matter where you are, there will be shadows. Don't worry about them." She lays her head on my chest and her hands are soft on my body. For a while, I do not think about shadows. It is good to be here, good to be with

217

this woman of my tribe, good to make love in the gray light. And the shadows are far away.

Then her head is resting on my shoulder and her arms are around me. Her breathing is soft and slow and gentle.

I think of Kirsten and the bear and the shadows in the city. It is so simple when Merle says it: the shadows are always there. I think of the Animal Master saying that he did not know what would happen on the Outside. Always, there are shadows.

"You're smiling," Merle says, and she traces the line of my lips with a finger.

I tell her of the shaman's drink and I tell her that I may not be strong enough to fight the bear and the shadows, but I will try.

"Tonight," she says and nods so that her head shifts against my shoulder. "Now, let's sleep."

I am glad to hold her. I feel like I am with my tribe again. At last, I sleep.

We awaken when the sun is high. I brew the shaman's drink in Merle's kitchen—in a pot on a stove. She has no sweathouse, but I use her shower and the steam is the same. When afternoon is coming to this world, I am ready.

We go to the city and the cold air beats against my face through the open window of the car. The air smells of smoke, of dust, of too many people in too small a world. We park in the street beside Corey's place just as the sun is setting.

The drink—still warm—is in a bottle that Merle calls a thermos. I drink from the bottle. I shiver as I swallow the bitter drink and the shadows press closer around me.

The world shifts. The gray street shimmers in the light of the setting sun. The air carries scents: rain, cement, smoke. But as the world shifts, I catch new smells on the breeze: fox, bison, deer, mammoth, wolf

218

and bear. I breathe deeply and look for a sign to show me which way to go. I am alert, ready.

The sunlight is gone and this world is filled with shifting shades of darkness. The street is flanked with gray shadows, tall as mountains. I move toward the darkness. The bear would seek darkness. She would not like the lights and cars and people.

I call to her through the darkness. In the Old Tongue, I call to her. "Come to me, Great One. We are not done with one another yet. Come to me."

"Where are you going, Sam?" asks a voice. For a moment, I am aware of Merle beside me, a slim shadow dressed in black.

I shake my head to shake away the darkness but it does no good. I must search for the words she will understand and I speak to her with an effort. "Do not ask. Just follow." And then she is gone in the darkness.

I know that this is not real darkness. I know that Merle can see the street before us and the buildings around us. I can taste the bitter drink at the back of my throat.

I see darker shadows in the mouth of another street and I turn that way. The air smells musty and the darkness shifts before me. A shadow lifts its antlered head. The gray shade of a buck in his prime tosses his antlers and stamps one hoof against the cement.

I have no spear. And a spear would do me no good against one such as this.

He grazed here once and now the grass is gone. "Are you lost?" I ask in the Old Tongue. "I can take you to a new home."

He comes for me, rearing up onto his hind legs, his sharp hooves lashing out. But I have dodged to one side and I lay a hand on his neck. I take him—easily and gently. And I remember the taste of new buds in the springtime. I know that I can run fast and far.

Shadows, many shadows, and the taste of the drink in my throat. I am running down a dark, dead street and a hawk, gray-winged and silent, swoops from the dark sky. I catch at her wing as she brushes by me and I take her. I remember soaring over the mountains and watching small creatures flee from my shadow.

I am running and a wolf runs at my heels—a gray shadow now, just as she was in life. I whirl to meet her when she lunges for me and I take her. And once I ran down deer in the forest and knew the taste of hot blood.

They have been waiting long, these spirits. Waiting and wandering in these empty streets. I take the bison and the mammoth; I take the fox and the cat; I take them and I am strong.

I call to the bear in the darkness. I call her a fool and I call her a coward. I run through the darkest streets and I call out to her, saying she is weak and stupid and slow.

The breeze carries the warm and musty scent of bear. Kirsten stands beneath a streetlight. She is waiting for me. The shadow of the bear towers over her. I stop, a few steps away from her.

"You want to find me, little man," says the she-bear in the Old Tongue. "You have found me." Her yellow eyes flash with anger and she reaches for me with a heavy paw.

I dodge her and the shadows swirl around us, darkness on darkness.

"You are a fool, little man," she says. "You should not have come here. I will eat you like a rabbit."

She drops to all fours and charges me, but I step aside. I hold the stone knife in one hand, though it will be no use against her. In the swirling shadows, I can see Kirsten and Merle, standing against a tall gray building. Merle's arm is around her daughter's shoulders.

The bear turns to follow me and I dodge again, but I trip over the curb, which is hidden in the shadows. I roll away from the bear's claws and the sound of her laughter.

"Fool," she is laughing. "You have no chance against me."

I scramble to my feet, ready to dodge again. "You are the fool, Great One." My voice is rough and I am short of breath. I am older than I was when I first dodged the bear's embrace.

"I am not the one who will lose, small shaman."

"You are wrong, Great One. You will beat me, but you will lose."

She shakes her head angrily and shifts her feet. Her claws scrape against the cement. "How will I lose?"

I take a step closer to her. "You take me and you will be alone in this world. You will stay here, forever alone."

She charges, and I am not expecting it. I can feel the wind as she passes close beside me. I whirl to face her again.

"I am alone now," she is growling. "What are you to me, little man? Two bites. No more."

"This is an empty world," I say. I gesture at the gray buildings around us. The air smells of bitter smoke; the sky is gray overhead. I cannot see the stars. "You have walked here. You know this world is empty."

"It is an empty world, but there is no other, little man."

"I know of another. A world filled with beasts."

She is watching me steadily now.

"I can take you there," I say.

"Why?" she growls. "Why do you say that you would take me? You could go alone."

I wave a hand at the sky, the buildings, the street. "The ones who built this world did not know the spirits, did not listen to them. We need you to help us protect our new world. We do not want to build a place like this."

Her eyes are angry and selfish. "You need me, little man."

I sheath my knife and glare back at her. "Just as you need me, Great One."

She snorts and tosses her head. "Still you fear me, little man. Do not think you are my equal."

"Fear you?" I grin at her and show my teeth. "No, Great One, I do not fear you." I tug on the claws that have hung around my neck for so long. The thong that holds them breaks and they come free in my hand. I cast the claws on the cement before her. I am strong with many spirits.

"You can come to the new world," I say. "Or you can be a fool."

I turn my back on the gray shadow and walk toward Kirsten and Merle. I can hear the bear's gruff breathing for a moment. I hear the click-click-click of her claws on the pavement. I can feel the soft warmth of her breath on my neck and I start to turn to face her. My hand brushes against her fur and then she is gone.

And I remember the taste of blackberries in the autumn and the sweetness of my mother's milk when I suckled in the den and the rotten scent of old logs when I overturned them to search for grubs. And I know the certainty of my own strength—but I do not know whether this certainty comes from me or from the bear. I do not know.

The shadows are gone. The bitterness is gone from my mouth. I stand in a circle of light beside a dark-haired woman and a dark-haired girl. "We will go," I say to them. And they follow me along the streets of this empty world, where shadows are only shadows.

This is the world of the Outside and we move quickly. This is the world I am leaving and all is well. We return to the Foundation. We return to Roy Morgan and Amanda—*dark*. Roy Morgan has prepared well for my return. We go to the large room, where words echo and the shadows are many.

The time has come and the air shimmers, just as it shimmered on a sunny day long ago. The old shaman is the first to step through the shimmering air. But I cannot think of him as old now—he is my age and I can match him gray hair for gray hair. He greets me as a brother.

How is it that my mother's eyes hold the same look as Amanda-*dark*'s eyes? I do not know, but I am glad to be in her arms.

My father, sister, uncles, aunts, cousins . . . all my people come to this place and gaze bewildered around the shadowy room. They are confused by the scents, the sounds, the strange people, as I was once confused.

But this is a different world; these are different people. Amanda-*dark* takes my mother's hand and smiles and my mother understands. Merle remembers a few words from the language of my people. "We are friends," she says to the shaman and the shaman stares in amazement. Kirsten touches the beads that hang around the neck of my small sister and they speak together, though neither understands the other.

It is a different world.

Roy Morgan works the Outreach and we can see the strange beasts grazing in an open meadow under a strange sky. The air shimmers before me and my people stand close around me.

I am strong like the bear, fleet like the buck, keen-eyed like the hawk. I am strong and my people will be strong.

"Now," says Roy Morgan and I step into the shimmering air. My people follow me. This world goes away. And a new world begins.

Headline books are available at your book-shop or newsagent, or can be ordered from the following address:

Headline Book Publishing PLC
Cash Sales Department
PO Box 11
Falmouth
Cornwall
TR10 9EN
England

UK customers please send cheque or postal order (no currency), allowing 60p for postage and packing for the first book, plus 25p for the second book and 15p for each additional book ordered up to a maximum charge of £1.90 in UK.

BFPO customers please allow 60p for postage and packing for the first book, plus 25p for the second book and 15p per copy for the next seven books, thereafter 9p per book.

Overseas and Eire customers please allow £1.25 for postage and packing for the first book, plus 75p for the second book and 28p for each subsequent book.